A Time to Lead

Author: Tony Sandora

I died one day and it changed my life forever.

Typically, all we know is what others have told us. We look

blindly into the faith

and assumed knowledge of what has been written before us. We

are taught to

trust in these truths and accept without question.

If we remain open minded, we can explore amazing depths

of the human

spirit. Think...my friend, look at people when you speak with them,

feel what they

feel and the world will open its' arms.

"Remember when you used to skip? When was the last time you skipped anywhere? Remember running to your father's arms? Jumping into the waiting arms of your father who couldn't wait to lift you high in the air and spin you around? The world spins as joy and happiness form a never ending, iron clad partnership with your every revolution. Remember that? I don't."

John sits in a brown leather chair that could use a few years of weathering to be considered comfortable. Back straight, legs crossed with his hands neatly cupping the end of the arms rests, pauses to illicit a response from the psyche doc de jour. "I see," says the Doc. John shifts position, leans forward with elbows on his knees and crosses fingers together in a prayer like position. "You see doc, its' not like it didn't happen, I just don't remember. Not like I have amnesia, I remember some stuff, flashes of memories," John's hands flitter about his face as if shooing away annoying gnats, "Its' very frustrating."

The hour is over, one he'll never get back. "I see," John mutters to his self as he reaches for the door handle to exit the *Foster and Fischer Medical and Wellness Center*, "do ya?" He feels it's all a waste of time and money. Rosy, John's secretary keeps making appointments and his respect for her is the only reason he keeps them. She has a good heart and genuinely cares for John's well-being. John feels there are some things you just have to accept.

Onward and upward, again…seriously…whose life is this anyway? Look up perpetual motion in the encyclopedia and there I am. All things considered, what is projecting me through all this cloud cover? John feels as if there a large, soft hand, quietly motioning him, directing him through a maze. He can see the maze, the twists and turns, the dead ends and no outlets all consist of the masses. He can see it more clearly than he can see the past. The vantage point is from above; the walls of this maze are thick. They are ten people deep. They stand in single file, shoulder to shoulder. They gaze silently into Johns' eyes. They don't speak. They can, they just choose not to.

"God", he whispered to himself, John stands in the parking lot of a soon to be rundown Cape Cod motel. It's 9am, where the hell did the building go? "Cape Cod in the off season, what a treat," John mutters to himself with one foot in a puddle and the other on dry pavement, he can barely make out a distant streetlamp through the fog.

$19.99… John stares at his brown loafers, gotta love those under twenty dollar specials at "The Mart" he thinks to himself. "The Mart", short for Walmart, "The BK Lounge", alias Burger King, "Maynerds", instead of Menards, what is the point of branding anymore. $40.00 Gap khakis, $20.00 work shirt from Overstock and a $60.00 t-shirt underneath it all, a gift last Fathers day from Aunt Franny, John does like the t-shirt best after all.

The parking lot is empty, where he stands, John feels like the only man in the world. The distant streetlamp displays this man's lonely world in a soft glow of compassion. When John pulled into this less than three star establishment on the previously clear evening, the office building was directly across the street. He remembers the moon last night, how bold and clear, somewhat daunting. He stood and stared, he remembers how it seemed to grow larger by the second. How it sucked him in, reduced all peripheral to non VIP status. Somebody could have walked up, said how ya do and punched him in the face without John even knowing they were there, funny…how life can get away from you like that.

This morning is a different story; the famous Cape fog has descended upon our hero. Here he stands, not far from the not so famous foot prints left from the night before, gazing upon our lone moon. "Can't see shit," says John and off he goes.

John is meeting with his commercial bankers this lovely morning. The credit line needs to be raised, terms need to be negotiated, blah, blah, blah, he thinks to himself. Is this what it has become? Have the youthful dreams of a glamorous life in big business, fame and fortune really come to this? Meeting with bankers? He now wonders if those dreams were his at all, seriously. It always seemed like traveling to meetings and carrying that fancy, expensive briefcase would be the coolest thing, well…they're not. Maybe to some I'm sure, but to John … not so much. He remembers snap shots, mental slideshows so to speak, at the airport or the mall…briefcases…they always seemed so impressive. John always wondered, what is in those things, super special important stuff had to be in those fancy briefcases.

As he walks through the hallowed halls fancy briefcase in hand, the mind never stops. I enjoy my life, he thought to himself, always believing there is more to life than money but not exactly knowing what that meant. Things have been laid out quite nicely for our boy John … But something is missing, now and then for no reason John gets an aching feeling in the midsection, a combination of nausea and vertigo. Always in control of his mental capacities, John has come to the conclusion he must concede victory to this ghost in his mind. There is no concern to him that it's' physical, he is a confident, athletic young man in his thirties. What could be wrong with a guy in his thirties, right? The mind is as complex as the universe itself and John is no fool.

As John makes his way through the reflective mist he thinks of his dad. John's dad was a home builder, apparently at the right place at the right time. He was a single family home builder that did most of the work himself, calluses, bloody knuckles and all. A housing boom and well-timed land purchases helped John's dad, Joe is his name, build a Midwestern developing empire. Things were good, the American dream and the perfect nuclear family. From what John remembers or was told, things were good.

Memories and stories are spurned from pictures and pictures and stories become memories, either way … we dearly hold on to both. Joe's dad met with an unexpected end when John was four. Thinking back, he is still not sure why or what happened. Does it really matter? An end is an end right? Or is it? John used to be concerned with this uncontrollable mind debate; nowadays he enjoys the competition with front row seats. What he does know for sure is mom was there and mom would sing, that is all that matters now.

   As he looks back, he thinks his dad would be proud, mom kept the business safe for him until he was old enough to learn the trade. Although he was never very good with his hands like his old man, he tried, he wanted to be … but it just wasn't there. He was good at managing however; he was good at negotiating too. That is where you find him today.

   "Well, I can't see her but I know she's there." John opens the door and settles in comfortably behind the steering wheel, he loves to drive and the pilot position in any car is a welcome place. The leather seats of the full size rental car that John upgraded thanks to the sweet girl at the agency are cool to the touch. This has a calming and refreshing feel this morning. "No time for breakfast today. Let's roll."

The glass building John is in provides full view of The Cape this morning, the sun is burning through the fog and clarity soon follows. John looks forward to the completion of this exercise and welcomes the sun on his skin. "Thanks, good doing business with you," says banker number 1, "Yes, I look forward to a lasting relationship", adds banker number 2. Handshakes and smiles all around, as John heads toward the elevators, relief disguised as satisfaction accompanies him.

With the meeting behind him, John sleepwalks through another rental car return and luggage check-in. Not surprisingly, the small print on the e-ticket confirms a layover in Dallas before L.A.'s destination is reached. Upon touch down in Dallas the salt air of the Cape has become a distant memory. As John removes his slightly battered black leather briefcase from below the seat in front of him he thinks to the weekend ahead. Work or play? John wonders. With Christmas coming up, maybe some shopping. These thoughts play themselves out as John exits the aircraft.

"Gate 7, good." He says to himself, the next gate is only a dozen gates away. John's next flight is in a couple hours, plenty of time to make the flight. Even so, a close gate provides mental comfort, given that, he decides to scout out Gate 7 before searching out a meal to hold him over until he gets to L.A.

On his mission John passes by "The Jet Rock", the sign reads, "Come on in, the bar is open." It's the holidays and the place is packed and quite jovial. John looks at his watch then looks back up. The grumble in his stomach provides a majority vote decides to take a seat. YEEEEEEEEEEEEHAAAAAAAAAAA! Shouts a potentially legal Texas bread male. Christine, a true blonde wearing a perfectly starched and pressed white shirt accompanied by slightly faded blue jeans turns to John and ponders, "What is the chemical reaction between testosterone and liquor that will make an adult act like that in public?" John, being a bit taken back by Christine's wide and wonderful blue eyes responds in kind, "I don't think he knows he's in public. We probably look like the herd, the bottles on the bar the cactus and the comings and goings of travelers are definitely the tumbleweeds, so technically … he is not responsible for his actions." John has a soft spot for pretty ladies, more of a sense of admiration than anything. With two hours left until flight time this opportunity is not to be missed. "That said, I don't think it's' safe for you here, want to take a walk?"

Without saying a word, a smile that rivals Christine's eyes tells John all there is. Not just yes, thanks I will take a walk, but hello, here I am, the women you've been longing for, the prescription for the internal vertigo. As Christine pushes back her chair and collects her coat and belongings, a lifetime passes, a lifetime of young and old, innocent and experienced, ignorant and jaded, past and present. Like floodwaters of realization, like but not quite what dad used to say, "kicked in the butt by the boot of reality", this is a different realization. This is joining the club, the club of people who experience the joy and pain of love. Like shopping with someone who doesn't know what they are looking for and saying things like, "I'll know it when I see it". It doesn't make sense but yet … there it is.

"You coming?" Christine's first words since the invitation, snapping John back into the 21st Century. "Without delay" he replies. John and Christine walk and they talk, they pass all people movers and navigate all last minute travelers. To the casual observer this couple has been friends forever and is certainly laughing over old times. John's hands are flailing around as he tells one of his favorite stories and Christine's eyes gleam as she responds in kind, friends forever indeed. Forever in this life is a relative term, you can never have too many forever moments. This forever moment lasted a mere 90 minutes, "To be continued." John pronounces to Christine as they must part to their final destinations. "Yes, to be continued." Christine responds in kind.

John stares and grins at the scuffed tray in front of him as the previous hour and a half are relived over and over while settling into coach. Business class is a luxury he can afford but rarely takes advantage. He will be in L.A. shortly, wishing he could call Christine but knowing it would be too soon.

#2 – Her first day

Its' a cold afternoon in Kansas City as Christine travels to her mother's house Christmas Eve day. Clean snow and crisp air, the kind of afternoon she remembers from her childhood. As Christine passes what the town referred to as "the snow bowl" she recalls countless hours spent with what seemed like the entire neighborhood at the sled hill by the river. A perfect row of neat houses on slim city lots, each with a perfect curl of white smoke reaching to the sky.

Christine is enjoying this Christmas break with an unusual zest this year. Teaching 3rd grade has always been a rewarding experience and spending time with family equally as rewarding. She'll admit it, she's not one of those independent, I can do it all type of girls. She has always relied on mom and dad for support and re-assurance. Christine has been able to rely on this because they have always been there with a sack full.

When she moved to L.A. for her first teaching gig, it was supposed to be a temporary move; she did not want to be that far from the comfort of her hometown. With a good job and Leave it to Beaver community, Christine is now a fixture in her small Los Angeles burb. Coming home this year has its' distinction, Christine is travelling with a remarkable sensation. There is no substance even the most genius or diabolical can create to manifest such emotion and long term effect comparable to an encounter between two human beings. This has happened; Christine knows it but has not recognized it. For those fortunate enough to have, they can still feel the soft glow to this day.

"Yes," remarks Christine, the streets are clean and dry in front of her childhood home. As usual, the driveway and sidewalk is clean and dry as well. Christine navigates her way toward the front door and looks upon her parents' home with an odd satisfaction. She has come to this home for most of her life. She has driven up to this house in the backseat of her parents' car and run up the driveway to the kitchen door countless times.

Parking on the street and entering through the front door instead of the usual kitchen entrance never fails to give Christine an unfamiliar perspective of a house she called home. The steel handle of the front screen door is cold and opens easily. A gentle "squeak" that every screen door in America welcomes each and every visitor is accompanied by the nasal sound of a snow blower from three doors down. Christine rests the screen against her backside as she opens the front door, "Hey mom, Merry Christmas!" Christine softly shouts down the hall to the kitchen, her mother quickly but cautiously puts down her kitchen utensils to greet her forever child at the door.

"Welcome home, darling" her mother lovingly says as she hugs her tight. "Where's dad?" Her mother replies "Out in his shop, working on his new toy, he'll be in shortly. Come sit, have some coffee and bring me up to date, you look wonderful!"

With a sincere appreciation Christine nods "Thanks mom, I think I met a guy." Intrigued and a bit confused, Christine's mother asks "What do you mean you *think* you met a guy? Is the nature of this individual's gender in question?" With a smile of a child and tilt of the head Christine has to wonder herself the nature of what she meant. "No, he is definitely a he, his name is John and he is from L.A. I met him at the airport on the way here. He … was wonderful. We talked and laughed, it was like I have known him forever, like we have been friends always." Christine is struggling to comprehend the combination of weirdness with the knowledge of absolute rightness. "I don't know mom, all I know is I am really looking forward to seeing him again, he is supposed to call me and we are going to get together."

The back door opens "Hey doll face" says an aged man stepping through the rear entry, "you look beautiful, Merry

Christmas." dad will always have the ability to make Christine blush.

#3 Judgment Day

It takes a lifetime to know someone
And only a second to say goodbye

The Holidays come and go too quickly, such an important time when family gets together for a wee few hours of redemption. People go out of there way to be nice to one another, stores are open until midnight … Utopia. They come and go and society gets back to normal.

We live together on a small planet without escape independent of one another … essentially. We have our groups or clicks of course, a billion groups of people all living together, our only interest in one another is the success or failure of another group and how it may affect our own.

Christmas with this group is over and Christine leaves the comfort of her parent's home to navigate the back roads to the airport when her cell phone rings. "Hello" Christine waits for her caller to speak.

"Hey doll face" says the caller. Christine is caught a bit off guard, "Dad?" says Christine quizzically.

The caller replies, "No, it's John … from the airport, I am sorry did I get you at a bad time?" John sitting on the counter in his kitchen makes a fist, looks at the popcorn ceiling and knocks himself on the head, doll face? Why would I call her doll face, I don't really even know this women. She is going to think I'm a nut job.

"Did you have a nice Christmas, mine was fine, I was hoping we could get together this weekend." John realizing he is babbling shuts up and awaits a response. His face is slightly red and the first regimen of sweat begins to assault the skin on his forehead. If he could see Christine's face he would know her answer, he would have his deja vu. He would see the face from the airport, the beautiful eyes and her glorious smile.

"That would be great, John, what do you have in mind." These are the words that generate an internal sigh and clearness of thought. John's face is back to his normal slightly tan color and the forehead retreat is on. After a short pause a confident voice replies, "I know this place, it's small and out of the way, I think you will like it." John was right, she would have liked it, of all the opportunities that befall a nice, middle class girl from the Midwest, this was not one of them. "It's a place called Rocco's, I will see you Saturday at six, that is ... if that works for you?"

"That works fine, John, I will see you then?"

"Check please!" It's Saturday and John is excited to leave the coffee shop and begin the short journey to Rocco's. Rocco's is a quaint little Italian joint John discovered one evening, it's not that great from the outside, but inside it is vintage Italian. Some old adages, not many, hold water indefinitely. You can't judge a book by its cover, no Rocco ... you cannot. As he begins the 15 mile stretch through the valley, his thoughts return to the day at the airport.

"Thank you" Christine receives her change from the women at the counter. She has been waiting for a good reason to pay $95.00 for a pair of shoes on a teacher's salary. "Looking good" she says to herself as she takes one last look in the tri-fold mirror before setting off on her date. The directions were simple, the man at Rocco's was clear and direct. Christine figures it will take less than

30 minutes, traffic not withstanding and begins her journey with 10 minutes to spare.

It is one of those days, here in L.A. A cool breeze is blowing through the valley today, picking up every scent like a kid on a shopping spree in a candy store. The sun is always in your face but never in your eyes and everyone is beautiful. One of those days where no one falls on their rollerblades, pulls a muscle pumping iron and the Bain De Soleil never runs out.

John turns the volume on his car radio to insane. "Jump back! … what's that sound? Here she comes, full blast and top down. Hot shoe, burnin' down the avenue. Model citizen … zero discipline" although not a Van Halen fan, his senses can't deny Eddie's riff. The stock stereo on John's black Cadillac is more than adequate to leave even the most angst of teenager ears ringing.

Three hours ago when John rolled up the sleeves of his blue button down and spent three minutes fixing his hair, a sense of peace and calm was at his side. John has spent most of his adult life attempting to follow in the footsteps of his father, trusting in the faith and belief he **is** following in the footsteps of his father. This has been more than a full time job, this is 24/7. Money was never the motivator, just a fortunate by product of hard work and good ethics.

John has always believed that when an opportunity presents itself, it's the end of opportunities efforts. It's time for the individual on the receiving end of opportunity to pick up the slack. This truth runs deep; John realizes life is full of opportunities … opportunities for money, love, happiness, grief and loss. Just as one of sane mind would not obsess with finding grief, one must not obsess with finding love. This sense of calmness arrives as John begins to feel the balance. "She's blinding, I'm flying, Right behind the rear-view mirror now. Got the feeling, power steering, Pistons popping, ain't no stopping now! Panama, Panamaha Panama, Panamaha!"…the music pauses… John sees a blinding light.

Christine emerges from a 90 degree curve to find herself in a sea of brake lights, a twisting snake with a hundred pairs of red, glowing eyes.

"No, please no, I do not want to be late, please." With no choice but to put her vehicle in park and justify the need for her headrest, Christine closes her eyes and sighs "Why today?" Christine digs through her purse for her cell phone and navigates the received call list. She will let John know she is running a bit behind. John's voice comes on the line, "Hi, thanks for calling, please leave a message and I will get right back."

"John, this is Christine, I am so sorry, but there is a backup on Topanga, I will be there as soon as possible, thanks for understanding, see ya in a bit … Hey, call me if you get this … thanks." Her feeling of self-pity for her plight turns to sadness for another as she gains ground on the culprit of this congestion. A log truck has reduced a black Cadillac to nothing but twisted metal and pieces of plastic.

John once again finds himself in a damp, foggy parking lot, the all too familiar streetlamp in the distance. This place is familiar, but somehow…unlike all others. Life is full of places that resemble a previous inhabited space somewhere in time, déjà vu right? Newly occupied space is by definition foreign, but the mind quickly identifies and relates ones viewable area to a preceding place in time, if only for the sake of sanity and the willingness to keep moving forward. John stands proud and upright in a parking lot that is undeniably a place he has been but at the same time completely and entirely foreign, how is that? Kinda like that crazy

Fourth of July party, when you pick up the weekends photos from the corner photomat. You don't remember shit but oh yeah, you still have the blister between your pinky toe and whatever the name is of that toe next to your pinky toe from the fireworks incident so conveniently captured by the one who told you so.

Nonetheless, here John stands. Knowing the surroundings and knows as a matter of fact that this place is Christopher Columbus territory. Unchartered land, for John at least.

He surveys this environment with assertive, steely eyes for he feels the unconscious need to be guarded. The feeling of deja vu is quickly masked by the realization he is neither cold from dampness nor warm from humidity. This creates an odd curiosity rather than a concern.

Before conscious validation of this lack of sensation can begin, John is approached by an unknown man. He wonders how this man could have approached so suddenly, in such a quiet setting as this, no birds, crickets or vehicles in the background. In fact, John can hear nothing at all and assumes when the strange man begins to speak, his words will fall on ears that have suddenly gone deaf.

"Hello John" says the man, a man of average stature, maybe 5' 10", wearing a black leather coat with the collar up and matching hat with the brim pulled down. The voice is calm with an inflection of your everyday good morning greeting at the office. John can see nothing else but the black cowboy boots beneath the full length leather and wonders if there is anything there at all. John says nothing and the man continues.

"Congratulations John, the name's Maxwell, but you can call me Max, I see you have done well for yourself. Business is good, future looks bright … but really, what have you got to show for it? Are you rich? Famous? Been voted the sexiest guy in America lately?

You got a minute? I think you do so I will continue as such, thanks." The polite morning how yah do has turned a bit sarcastic, thinks John. "I have a proposition for you; we need a guy like you on our team. Pay is double what you bring in these days; fringe benefits are a premium John, P-R-E-M-I-U-M!" Max declares as if howling at the moon. "The potential for fame is tremendous and benefits include all the plastic surgery you can withstand.

"I am not so sure about this" says John.

"Oh, just hear me out buddy." Max continues. "It's more or less a sales type position; you would use your logic and influential personality to convince others our way is the best way. We would support you no matter WHAT! Give you all the necessary tools, all we ask is you use all means available to make the sale. You must not be afraid to deceive just a bit, maybe even lie a little. No big deal, its' just a means to an end. Our latest polls show people liked to be lied to anyway. What do you think?"

John thinks those must be exit polls but decides to keep that to himself. In a soft voice, it is John's turn, "That does not sound very honorable" he replies.

"HONOR!" Yells Max, seeming to grow larger with every word. "What does honor have to do with ultimate success? Do you think the guy with the foot on your back on his way up the latter is thinking about honor! Think again my man; honor is for fools and losers. Don't be so righteous, nobody likes righteous people; in fact, there is no such thing as a righteous person, just someone pretending to care about others to get ahead. Now come on man, come with me and let's have some fun." Even though the man in black now appears to be seven feet tall, John does not waiver, if anything John is a man who will stand on his convictions no matter what the battle.

"No thanks," John replies, "I have known many an honorable person, honorable and righteous. It's not that complicated, there are a lot of people who just try to do what's right, be honest and not judge others. To me, that's an honorable person. I think I will take a pass."

"You disappoint me John," states Max, "I don't like to be disappointed." With that, the faceless man in black faded into the fog, never turning away from John. John could swear he faded away without taking a single step.

Christine pulls up to the valet at Rocco's, the green numbers on the dashboard clock are telling her she's now 20 minutes past their agreed upon meeting time. Christine is concerned she is late but still struggles with the emotions of the loss she witnessed on the way here. Somewhere … someone is not returning home today. Somewhere … someone is getting the worst news imaginable. Christine wonders why things have to be this way.

Running late, she does not hesitate to pull up to valet, she gives the valet guy two bucks and makes her way to the entrance. There is wrought iron and wood all around but no sign of John.

Christine scans the tables for John, it's not much of a challenge, considering there are maybe twelve tables in the quaint little dining area. Christine sighs deeply as she looks back towards the door then up to the bar area. She instinctively heads toward the bar, which is where people wait, right?

The heavy wooden bar speaks of old world, a time when cell phones and automobiles didn't exist. These ancient times lacked technology but contained an equal amount of pain. Christine simultaneously runs one small hand through her blonde hair, off her flawless face and pulls back a wood framed steel backed stool with her free hand. As Christine takes a seat in this land between then and now, the bartender greets her kindly.

"Can I get you something Miss?" asks the bartender. "Not yet, thanks" Christine is hoping John, perhaps needed a restroom break and will return in a moment. From her seat at this vacant bar, she hangs desperately to the hope each patron who rounds the corner is her date for the evening.

Several minutes pass and the bartender continues on his quest, "Are you sure I can't get you something miss?"

"Sure, thanks, a glass of Chardonnay would be fine." While the bartender busies himself, Christine reaches in her purse for her cell phone, flips it open to see no missed calls. A few touches of the buttons and Christine immediately gets John' voicemail and hangs up without delay. There will be no more calls to John; there will be no more voicemails. Christine takes a sip of her Chardonnay and will be alone for the rest of the evening.

Christine enters the abyss of the unknowns and what ifs. She fondly recalls the encounter with John at the airport and manages a sideways grin. It now seems years ago and somewhat surreal, as if she watched the episode unfold on the television during a light night showing of an old black and white. This is apparent in her mind as well as her soft face, the seasoned bartender gently puts his hand on the bar and tells Christine her Chardonnay is on the house.

"Hey JC," John has not been called JC since his mother died, she was only thirty three. When John was a very young boy, each and every night his father would read him a bedtime story and rub his head for comfort so he could fall to sleep. These stories were about pirates or cowboys, Dinosaurs or race cars, this detail mattered little much, but what did matter was each and every night the last thing John needed was a kiss on the head from his mother. After this kiss, his mother would always whisper, "Sleep nice JC, happy dreams my boy." The big picture feels so vague but the details so crystal clear.

Once again the voice says, "JC, can you hear me?" John turns in slow motion to see the women behind the words, frightened to the core of what he may find. What he finds is no different than what anyone would find if they were to enter one of a thousand office buildings and walked into one of a million offices.

A smartly dressed woman with smart hair and smart shoes stands before John with hands neatly folded in front of her, toes pointed ever so slightly apart. What else, thinks John, what else did I think I would find in a foggy parking lot in the middle of God knows where, with no birds or crickets or cars and calling me JC.

"I can hear you fine, thanks. I was just a little startled when you called me JC, only my mother called me JC. Peculiar don't you think?"

"My name is Angela" says the women, "It is nice to meet you, can I have a minute of your time?"

John replies with a jest like sarcasm "Are you gonna get huge and pissed off if I say no?"

"I think not," says Angela. "I am sorry for the way you were treated by Maxwell. I am sad to say we are in similar industries but trust me, different philosophies … I have a proposition as well."

John is compelled to interrupt but remains respectful and polite, "I don't remember putting a resume on line, what's with all the job offers? I like what I do, granted it's not the most exciting job in the world but it puts food on the table of 35 families, it also provides health care and a few bennies to those same families. So what gives?"

"We give." Angela replies, "We offer hope when all seems lost, we challenge the proud when their pride has been stripped, we give love to the lonely. We are the origin of our industry. What would you say if I told you, you could be an integral part of our business plan … and guarantee your current employees would be well taken care of? Better yet, why don't I just show you."

4 Heaven 101

Angela did not give John a chance to agree or disagree. As Angela's last words were spoken, she passed one hand across the face of John, when that hand returned to the side of his new found friend; John' surroundings were once again unfamiliar.

Familiar in a sense of structure and layout, commercial carpet and industrial tile on the floors, better than average lighting and the cleanest cubicles John has ever seen. Funny thing though … no windows. Not knowing why, John follows Angela without word through this labyrinth of normality. Emerging from this labyrinth like two victorious explorers, Angela stops short of a large double door.

Angela and John pause before this door, John turns back to take a look at the bustling office behind him. As he looks around he notices everyone seems abnormally cheerful. Not crazy happy like they just hit the lotto with their office pool and everyone is happily drafting their resignations, no…just cheerful and content.

John turns back to view the door and then to Angela. The pair see eye to eye, John does not have to look up or down to address his guide. "Well" John inquires, "I am sorry but I don't have all day, it currently escapes me but I believe there is someplace I need to be."

"Belief is a touchy subject these days John." says Angela, "As for needing to be someplace, quite the contrary, allow me." Angela gives a gentle push and the large double doors swing open with ease. Beyond these doors is a room of rich woods and plush carpet, deep colors and even deeper grains. John thinks the table in the center of this goliath room must have a thousand coats of lacquer. As they move further into the room from the corner entrance John looks skyward. The ceiling appears infinite, there are mirrors bordering the ceiling and John assumes it to be some sort of optical illusion, a twisting cascade of blue sky and puffy clouds that extend beyond comprehension, an illusion indeed.

A moment before this spectacle causes John to lose his balance; he looks back toward Angela and shakes it off. He continues to follow Angela to the monster table.

There he can see four stewards standing silently, one at each corner of the brilliant table.

"Please have a seat" Angela requests as she moves towards the table. Fifty or so ornately carved wooden chairs with eight foot high backs surround the table, John has no idea how he will even move one of these chairs let alone take a seat in it.

As the Angela and John approach the table the four stewards converge, each one neater than the next. John thinks these people must have the best dry cleaners on the planet for he has not seen a wrinkle since he got here.

"Thanks" says John in a politely uncomfortable manner as the stewards assist with his seat. The stewards respond in kind to Angela, now the two sit comfortably next to each other in this grand room, at this grand table.

John feels infinitely tiny, like a small bird in a large tree sitting on the edge of the Grand Canyon.

"Where am I?" inquires John for the first time. John is coming to the realization this is really, really strange. The foggy parking lot, the odd man Angela referred to as Maxwell, and let's not forget Angela herself.

"You're dead." these words flow from Angela as simply as the answer to one plus one equals two? The silence returns, the deafening silence from the foggy parking lot has returned. Some people say your life flashes before your eyes when you die, this is true for some, but the truth for all is you may see something but you will hear nothing when you confront the images of the actual experience itself.

John takes a moment, he pauses, is allowed to recall the last moment of his life in the safety of this chamber, he doesn't see what is going on outside this room in the formerly cheery, bustling office sanctuary. In fact, there is no idle chit chat, there are no copiers running and not a soul has tapped the "print" icon. Everyone is sitting quietly with there heads bowed in respect for John and his quest for rationale for they have all been there themselves.

The exchange goes something like this:

John: "Dead?"

Angela: "Yes, dead."

John: "Dead?"

Angela: "Yes … dead."

John: "As in deceased?"

Angela: "Yes."

Angela gets the idea this could go on for an eternity, as fun as it sounds for it is an eternity that is available to them, she interrupts the festivities.

"Yes John! You know what happened, the truck, the logs, the whole thing. I know you know, if you need time I can give you that, if you are OK, please ... let me know and we can move on to the business at hand."

John is in a new place, prior to the last two minutes John was in a familiar place, this place was an office. This place was any other place, this place was on planet Earth for starters. There are times when you feel you are in control, times when you feel comfortable in your surroundings and the friends you are with. Then all of a sudden, something happens, this place or person you thought you knew changes followed immediately by an uncomfortable feeling and compulsion to make a hasty exit.

What kind of change you ask? A colossal, monumental, three hundred and sixty degree head spinning, scientifically impossible change. Some people might cartoon it up as jaw dropping with eyes buggin' out, but unlike cartoons, this is real. The funny thing is, it was always there, you just didn't know it, you just didn't see it. Comprehension is like sifting through the rubble of truth, dust notwithstanding.

There John stands, amongst the rubble with nothing left but questions and uncertainty.

"Then where am I?" John poses.

"Where else?" Angela replies, "but in Heaven ... you have been a good person, you haven't killed anybody, you've gone to Church ... on Holidays, given to the needy, stuff like that ... trust me John, you've made your sacrifices and by all means where else would you be?"

John stares down on the table they are seated, as he ponders the situation he taps all four fingers on the table. One finger immediately following the other, pinky to index finger, over and over on the mirror finish.

John is getting a bit more comfortable in his surroundings and ponders, "That's it? I'm not one to look a gift horse in the mouth but ... I have my regrets, things I've done."

Angela intercedes, "Regrets are not for what you've done but for what you've failed to do. We are designed to live and react to our surroundings with no intentions of perfection. Don't regret the actions you have taken in your life John, it is not regret which damns, it is the intentional imposing of suffering on others that will lead to judgment."

"Then what do you mean by the business at hand?' John wonders.

"Well,' Angela adds, "We need someone of your expertise, you see, we have a position of importance that must be filled and you are highly regarded."

#5 How about the signing bonus?

John begins to accept the once impossible but requires additional information, "Ok, I accept the fact that I have been a decent, albeit not perfect person during my lifetime and I have been graciously rewarded with eternal life. Although I am still not sure what you mean when you say I've made my sacrifices."

"Is this it? This doesn't seem much different than Earth. Where are the pearly gates? Where is my babbling brook and song birds? I don't mean to be ungrateful but this is not what I expected. You're real nice and everything, but this is Heaven? By the way, what did you mean when you said I was regarded for a position of importance?"

It is now Angela's turn and John cannot wait. "First off, you are not actually in Heaven per se. You are in what is referred to as Heavenly Headquarters, this is where it all happens and all has happened, if you know what I mean."

John is now more puzzled than ever. "This is where we manage creation. Heaven, my dear is down the hall and to the left. Typically, a recently deceased that ascends to Heaven does not get the dog and pony show such as you did. Typically it is white lights, harps and such, then joining with the rest of Heavens inhabitants. It is quite spectacular actually. Upon arrival they gain an understanding of how it all works but with that understanding is an acceptance that things are taken care of by management."

"Management?" John asks. "So you manage the workings of Heaven from this office?"

"No dear." Replies Angela. "This is Heaven, it is perfect, we must manage all of creation. That which is not perfect, that which is continually challenged by evil. Let me help you understand, creation is much larger than Earth and Earths inhabitants. It is however, a large project and one which our Chairman keeps a close eye on."

John realizes he has been speaking in two word sentences but cannot help himself. "The chairman?" John asks. "Who is the Chairman?"

Angela replies in kind. "You would know him as God, among other things. He is the Chairman of the Board, he is the ultimate creator and designer and has final say in all activities. You know me as Angela of course, but I am also the operations manager for Earth. It is the most challenging and rewarding of all projects and I need your help."

John is trying to perceive the concept of Heaven being so similar to a corporate structure on Earth. "I'd hate to be in one of your budget meetings." He unknowingly says aloud with a chuckle.

"Excuse me?" says Angela.

"Nothing, just thinking aloud, how can I help, I mean, where would I fit in?"

Angela returns to where she left off in her explanation. "I, I mean we … need a new supervisor in our Department of Human Affairs or DHA. Our leadership in that area has been inadequate for quite some time and I must say in need of serious overhauling.

You would be working closely with the other departments of the Earth Project."

John once again and almost positive it will not be last time interrupts Angela again. "Ok, DHA, I am afraid to ask what the other departments are, but please, do go on."

Angela continues. "the other departments consist of wildlife or DWA, plants or DPA and last but not least, research and development which was originally DRDA but we lovingly call them Doctor DA, don't worry, you will get a chance to meet them."

Angela finally gets a chuckle of her own. "So you see, we have separate departments overseeing the entire planet project which consists of humans, plant life, animals and research and development. Pretty simple, don't you think? These departments are supposed to work together for the good of the whole, but I am sorry to say, the lack of good supervision has caused a riff between DHA and ALL the other departments. The result has been staggering and if the problem is not rectified soon it may be too late."

"You think I might be able to help." says John. "You want me to supervise the DHA. What happens if I politely turn down the position?"

Angela sighs, this is the first time John has seen the softer side of her. "You will join the others in the Kingdom of Heaven and begin your afterlife. But I am afraid newcomers will be fewer indeed, yes quite a bit fewer."

#6 Please to meet you, won't you guess my name

Is does not take long for John to let Angela know what he has known all along. "I would love to give it a try, Angela. I am still not sure why you have chosen me, wasn't Howard Hues available? That guy could shake things up or how about Ronny, you know Ron Reagan, now you're talking."

Angela finds this all too amusing. "John, these guys are busy, Earth isn't the only project you know. I am glad you have decided to work with us, let's get going shall we."

With that comment the steward's slide John and Angela's chairs back. Angela leads John to the opposite end of the room, up seven stairs to yet another mammoth size double door. Funny, John doesn't remember seeing these doors when they first entered the room.

They open with ease, John and Angela emerge to a room filled with computer stations and large monitors, in the center of the room is a huge screen with the words Central Command written across it. Although John has never been, this is what he would imagine NORAD would look like. Not a huge room, the space is used to perfection. From the entrance, to the right, only a few steps down is a working environment with several workstations in a circle. As John looks closer, it appears to be four workstations, with multiple monitors at each, looks like three monitors each. Yes, John confirms to himself, twelve large monitors in a circle in the center of the room.

On the monitors John can see images of Earth, of people going about there daily business. Monitoring the monitors are four ordinary but young looking individuals, two male and two female as John looks on. They look up briefly to John and Angela and then return to the business at hand, intently viewing these images and often clicking from one set of images to another.

John follows Angela up a small set of stairs to the left that leads to an open a hallway that overlooks and surrounds the entire floor. Along this hallway is a series of doorways on one side and a steel rail on the other. John counts four, three along the hall and one at the end, this door is different it is a double door. Angela opens the first and leads John inside. "This is your office John, get comfortable you have a meeting in fifteen minutes."

John immediately gets that feeling in his stomach. A feeling of dread mixed with excitement and nervousness. John has always been a social fellow but was thrust into the world of public relations and presentations when he came of age. He loved doing it and was quite successful at it, but there was always that same feeling. It is with him now and will be until this first introduction is behind him.

"Thanks for the prep time Ange" John remarks. "Will you be joining me?" As Angela proceeds to exit John new office she has these departing words. "I will introduce you to the other department supers, but after that, I have complete confidence. See you in fifteen." and she is off.

John takes a look around, nice modern desk made to look old world and a big chair. Steely but warm grey tone on the walls is comforting. The desk has a standard looking keyboard, no mouse though. It all looks pretty typical but not a single wire anywhere. On the wall is a large monitor with the words "password please" in large letters.

John takes a seat to address his new digs. He now sees the keyboard has a built in roller ball just below the arrows and to the right of the keys. He gently runs his fingers over the ball to move the curser on the screen. It feels good, there is just the right amount of friction, the left and right "click" is just below this roller ball.

John looks back up to the screen and types in his usual password m-a-s-o-n, the same password he has used for years, the name of his German Shepard companion from his childhood. After a short pause and a shrug John hits enter and is not surprised to see the screen come to life.

On the screen are several icons, these icons consist of <u>choose location</u>, <u>saved locations</u>, <u>hot spots</u>, <u>favorites</u>, <u>inbox</u> and <u>search box</u>. With all that has happened since John's untimely ascent, one image has returned to his mind's eye with crystal clearness. With that …and one index finger… C-h-r-i-s-t-i-n-e, is carefully typed in the search box. John looks at the enter button, makes a rising loop with his hand and taps the enter key.

There is Christine, high definition times a thousand. She is sitting in her car at a stop light in LA. It's just her face, he could sit here for hours, maybe even days, the way he feels now, an eternity would be just fine. She sits in solemn silence; the sun as well as John is behind her now.

There is no clock in the room but somehow John knows he has exactly seven minutes until his meeting, not enough time to get too deep on this system and decides to take a walk down the hall to check out his new facility.

"OK" John says to himself, "Sorry doll face, sorry for everything, this will have to wait, let's see what's behind door number two." The first door in this series is not surprisingly a DHA Meeting Room, this is boldly stamped to the placard on the wall next to the door. John turns his head ever slightly as not to be too unobvious that he is trying to hear through the door, nothing, no sounds emanating from this room. The next door is the rest room, John considers this as conveniently located but wonders if it is male or female. The last door is the large double, no time to put an ear to this one as Angela emerges from it.

"You ready?" asks Angela.

"Sure" replies John, "but I need to use the rest room first." Angela, always being courteous motions to the door just behind them. John inquires "Is this the men's or ladies room?"

Angela responds quickly. "It is both, you don't know it yet but you have left your shame at the door. It is not something you realize is gone when you are rid of that nasty emotion. Go ahead, take care of business for we have other business at hand."

"No pun intended?" remarks John.

After a short pause Angela replies with a giggle. "No John, no pun intended."

Angela leads John back through the double doors. This set of doors leads another hallway quite similar to the one they just exited. This time when they approach the meeting room, the door is open and occupied. Angela enters the room quite confidently and John follows, but not too closely.

John has been around the block a time or two and he sub consciously enters into business mode. If John follows Angela too closely it may be perceived as what John refers to as "puppy doggin," it is important to make a good first impression and John does not want to be taken for a lap dog.

Although the conversation up to this point has been quizzical John is all too aware of the magnitude of his undertaking. He hasn't shown it but his mind has been racing since his comprehension and acceptance of this task. He remembers his life on Earth, he knows how messed up things are. He now recognizes the balancing act that the human race is in the midst of.

John is seeing more clearly the struggle between good and evil and the struggle for the survival of sanity amongst the unknown. John recalls the story of Adam and Eve and the punishment for defying God. As the story goes, the punishment was awareness. Adam and Eve banished from the Garden of Eden now recognizing they are naked and susceptible to emotions such as greed and vengeance.

To John, the biggest punishment is love, not just love, the joy true love brings is immeasurable. The punishment is love combined with the inevitable … loss. For some, they do not have the ability to enjoy the true nature of boundless love because they are accompanied by the terror of the possibility of a tragic loss. Such is our fate.

Although John has no false sense of being able to change this, he recognizes the potential to make things better and is willing to spend eternity in the process.

"John," Angela begins the introductions, "This is Jonah, Jonah is the acting supervisor for the department of Nature. Next to Jonah is Noah, Noah is the acting supervisor for Animals, Noah has extensive experience is this area and has been leading this department for quite some time, haven't you Noah. Last but not least is Geraldine, she is our master research and development guru.

Everyone, this is John, as you have been told, he is our new supervisor at the DHA. John, I leave you in good and well experienced hands, if you require assistance of me, please do not hesitate to call. Good luck to all." At that, Angela removes herself from the merriment.

John immediately takes the opportunity to extend a warm welcome himself. "Hello and thanks for the opportunity, this has come up quite suddenly for me but I am honored to be working with this group. Angela has been gracious enough to show me around but I still require some additional time to get a handle on the operations end of this. I appreciate your patience in this matter and I feel there is an immense amount of improvement that can be made by the DHA for the good of the whole project. I also understand the importance of everyone and everything working as one and will do my best to make the necessary improvements."

After a short pause, Noah speaks. "John, your pleasantness is well taken, am I to observe that by your words you mean to begin this relationship as an ally to the good cause of Earth?"

"Yes." Replies John. "I am committed to the good cause of Earth and all that resides upon it."

Noah continues. "John, if I may, that which resides is that of continuous change, forces that exist on Earth exist for the sole purpose of existence. So that you may understand, a child is born, this child would and could not survive if change did not immediately begin. The forces of change have been put in motion for the survival of the child. Earth and all that resides **is** our child John, embrace the change and while you have your fingers firmly in this embrace, do all that is within your power to point this child in the right direction."

John nods in understanding. "Thanks everyone, there is no time like the present." Noah, Jonah and Geraldine nod in approval and wish John well.

#7 Round two

John returns to his office as the conversation from the initial meeting with the other supervisors runs through his head.

"Hey boss." John turns to view the source of this greeting. He turns and is surprised to see four individuals in a perfect line behind the greeter. Well, four total including the greeter. They are in such a straight line John must peer around the greeter to get a glimpse of the rest of this crew. He recognizes this group from earlier, these are the faces at the workstations in the circle.

Extending a hand the greeter continues "Hi, I'm Becky." John first impression is that this has got to be a mid-west girl. Her round face and wide smile scream of country.

"Hello Becky," he replies. "Nice to meet you, does your tail have a name?" As she steps to the side to introduce the next in line Becky casually pushes back her long, tightly curled brown hair.

"This is Patrick." Becky introduces a mid sized, John guesses about five foot seven or eight, stocky, firm lipped wild eyed creature masking himself as a mid twenties lad.

"Hey," Says the lad with a nod as he shuffles to the side.

Becky continues on, "This is Mike and then Jennifer."

John recalls back to his high school years, he remembers that one kid whose parents had a lot of money and made sure everyone knew it. How that kid had tried so hard for people to like him by wearing cool clothes and acting like he thought people wanted him to act … how the cool kids acted.

John remembers this kid, he remembers that he was a decent kid that would have found a place if he would have let the world know who he really was. This Mike is one of those kids.

The last to be introduced is Jennifer, John is certain on Earth Jennifer's license plates read "i m jen". There's innocence on her face and is quite certain she has a big heart to go with the big hair.

"Becky … everyone," says John." For what do I have the pleasure?" Becky appears to be the leader of this ensemble; she is put together and maintains just the right amount of perkiness for the job. "Sir, we are your leads, we are the liaisons between you and the floor."

"The floor?" John inquires.

"I am sorry, yes the floor, where we follow the trends and the hot spots to determine what action is to follow."

John snaps his fingers and commands, "Follow me please." He proceeds to the meeting room of the DHA, Becky and her tail in tow. "If you are my leads then it is with you I begin. I am going to require a brief but precise description of the day to day activities here… and how on Earth or the lack of being on it do we accomplish our goal of counter acting Evil, criminals, wrongdoers, hate mongrels, party crashers, bad hair days and reality TV?" John realizes he has just wigged out a bit but feels it is just. "Really people, I need a rundown, who would like to start?" John was looking at Becky as he ended the rather abrupt statement, somehow he assumed this was appropriate.

Becky swings her head to position her natural curls to the left side of her round, partially freckled face, she purses her lips and raises her eyebrows as she awaits the conclusion of John's current proclamation.

"Well … we have the ability to monitor all that occurs on the planet. Of course that is far too great a task to monitor everyone, so our system is set up to monitor certain individuals that we target.

"How do we identify a target? Asks John.

"We recognize targets by what we call hot spots. When there is unusual activity around one individual we begin to monitor this person. For example, if we notice a trend of one person lashing out against others or abusing animals and such, we decide if this person is susceptible to outside influence. We hope to counter act or deter the behavior escalating to something more dangerous or harmful.

"How do we counter act anything from up here?" inquires John.

Becky continues. "I'll get there, we start out by monitoring vitals, if the heart rate or blood pressure escalates, we get an alarm and a pop up. We can then go to view mode and determine if action should be taken."

John finds this all too fascinating. "What type of action?"

This time Patrick explains. "This morning, we identified a potential situation. We had a pop up on a guy we were tracking. This guy had a ton of priors, been in and out of jail for some small stuff, a real potential interrupter.

"Interrupter? What's an interrupter"

Jennifer is seated at a chair alongside John's desk, she is wearing a white shirt with light, lime looking vertical stripes and a just above the knees pink skirt. She is leaning forward on the chair with her hands neatly folded on her lap, knees touching. Her feet are wrapped around the legs of the chair, toes to the floor and heals to the sky.

"An interrupter is just that." Says Jennifer.

John, seated in his chair just to the left of Jennifer takes one fluid motion to lean forward, fold his hands and turn to her for this explanation.

"We call then interrupters because that is what they do, they interrupt life. They interrupt happiness, they interrupt well being," Jennifer is now getting a little worked up, "they interrupt … well … everything that is good in life!"

"OK, I get it, thanks Jen." John looks back toward the rest of the crew and sits back in his chair, elbows resting on the chair arms, fingers crossed and thumbs together. "Ok, so you have this potential interrupter …"

Patrick continues. "So what happens is, his heart rate shot up so we went to view mode. We noticed he was concentrating on a women across the street and determined action should be taken. We quickly panned out to get a broader view.

Patrick pauses for a moment, "Let me backtrack a bit, we can't make people **do** anything, everyone makes decisions based on their own free will. What we **can** do is put certain thoughts into their heads, but we have to be very careful, if we put thoughts into an overly unstable individual it could have the opposite result, send them over the deep end if you know what I mean.

Anyway, we identified a couple … a husband and wife. They were driving in their car and approaching our interrupter from down the block. Our data showed they were from out of town and looking for a specific address, we quickly put a simple sense of doubt into the man's head and an urgent feeling to take a sharp left when his wife was telling him he was supposed to go right. The thing is, when this happened the wife got frustrated, as you could imagine and made the man pull over immediately and ask directions.

When they inquired about directions it was with the guy we were tracking, this was enough to distract the man and the woman who was the potential victim went on her way."

"Is that it?" queries John. "Babysitting? I see we are talking about modifying human interaction … but is that our jobs, interrupting the interrupters? My understanding was the human populace is kind of relying on us to help them in the often overwhelming struggle between good and evil. Listen Becks," John has a bad habit of changing or deleting letters from peoples' names, "you may have forgotten but there is a lot of bad stuff going on down there. People have doubt, people are afraid of their neighbors, nut jobs are going on shooting sprees, there has to be more than this."

Becky replies, "You're the boss John, you tell me." Becky excuses herself from the group, she doesn't remove herself completely, sort of taking the moon position in this newly created solar system and John is Earth.

John looks at Patrick with wonder, "What's up? What is Becks bent about?" "Well," Patrick explains, "It sort of complicated."

Mike has been leaning in the doorway this entire time, listening to the conversation with his shoulder on the door jam and his hands in his pre-washed style jeans pockets. John notices his RonJon t-shirt is perfectly pressed and the RonJon logo, "one of a kind" has not faded even one bit. Mike finally, completely enters the room. "She doesn't have any … experience if you know what I mean."

"No," replies John, "Please enlighten me." Patrick continues. "Becky has been raised here, she has spent no conscious time on Earth, that is … she was what we call a "lost" baby. Her mom lost it, when she was born she trashed Becky in a dumpster. She has been raised in heaven and does not have the experiences you made note of. Not that it's a bad thing, she just can't relate."

"Understood." replies John.

#8 Some things are meant to be

Becky has returned to her workstation, she is seated with her back to John's office in front of three flickering screens. John motions to the three remaining to follow him as he leaves his office and heads down the open hallway to the stairs that lead to the work area. They silently follow.

"Well, let's get busy, if we had a concept of time we would be wasting it, but we don't so let's … just … get busy. Hey Becks!" John calls out from the last stair. All four pause for a moment as John calls out Becky's name. They stand in a row on the stairs, each one with their left foot resting on one step and their right foot on the step above. Their left hand on the steel rail and heads all turned to Becky. Becky looks at them and laughs, almost positive that at any moment she'll hear them break out in "Sergeant Peppers Lonely Hearts Club Band."

John is pleased to see Becky smile and does not question the root of her amusement. John stops and puts his hands on his hips in front of the three monitor work station next to Becky.

"OK, I understand the monitoring thing, are there any other ways to interact or help people? What are we dealing with, if we are counter acting evil, how is the evil so prevalent? Are their rules different from ours?"

"No." As Becky explains, Patrick, Jennifer and Mike take a seat at their workstations. "They have a better publicist, it is called *the media*. There is a ton of love and good in the world, far outweighing the evil, it is really the faith that is lacking. Trends show that this can and has led to dangerous levels resulting in action from the big man. I believe that is why the change in management around here. Things have gotten screwed up, previous management was strictly old school and not forward thinking."

Becky's eyes turn away from John and back to her monitors. On her desk to the right of her keyboard, mouse combo unit is a glass container with a large glass handle. On the side of the glass in big red letters are the words, *If you can read this cup, you're too comatose.* John is glad to see sense of humor can survive even if his body can't, sarcastic humor and all. He figures if this day job doesn't work out, he can get a job at the glass factory. He can see it now, his cup can say, *my other car is a hearse.* John shakes his head and laughs.

Becky looks back up at John to see what is so funny. With no evident funny business going on, she continues with her explanation. "You see, the monitoring is basically quality control. Previous management has issued certain guide books, you see, as a rule … we can insert inanimate objects at our discretion. So …

these guide books were meant to be used by the current civilizations they were introduced to as teaching tools. As the world evolved and changes took place, people evolved as well. This was a long time ago, at the time these guide books were inserted the world was a much different place. The books and the teachings were all basically the same, teachings of love, compassion and patience. Each sector or geographical location of the world was given a teaching that could be understood by the people it was intended to be found by…and it was. But none of the original teachings or the founders and followers of the original teachings are around anymore, only fragmented versions remain and current societies intellect wouldn't understand it if it did remain. The teachings were not literal, people didn't think that way back then. Anyhow … the good thing is the teachings created a revolution. This revolution remains today across the continents. Evil has tried to distort the original teachings and has an army continuing to do so … such is the nature of existence.

"You'll have to bring that one up with the big guy." John is steady and Becky thinks … hopes she can see the wheels turning. "Inanimate objects, OK" … as he speaks, John begins to shake his head a bit, as if agreeable with something, "monitoring … OK."

John looks down and points to Becky's mug. "Can I get a sip of that? I'm parched."

"Sure." Agrees Becky as she pushes the mug closer to John with the back of her hand.

John spins the mug to get to the handle side. "Thanks, what is it?"

"Just water"

John inserts two fingers into the handle and lifts the mug shoulder high, before taking a drink he turns to Becky. "Sure could use a hot cup of Joe right now, used to stop at this place with the best Kenyan blend around."

Becky looks at the mug and back to John. John looks at the mug … then back to Becky.

"Cool." Says John matter of factly. John lifts the mug to his nose to take in the warm, pleasing scent of his fresh, hot, newfound mug of Kenyan coffee…nice.

"When I was on Earth," continues John, "if we needed something accomplished we would send in the *team*. Whether it was sales, technicians or whomever, if there was a problem, we sent in our team to fix it. We need to get our group together and set up a team to get things on track, first let's …"

Becky politely interrupts this process. "John, sorry to interrupt but, like anything, there are rules. With objects, they are what we design. The only rule there is it must be found and not given. We do decide on the location though. Another big thing is, although we can physically go to Earth from the afterlife there are complications here. A couple things, we do not choose our form on Earth, this is random and is quite risky. Most importantly, we are not allowed a second chance. If we choose to go back, remember, this is a choice, once here in the kingdom we are never forced to go back, but if we do choose to go back and something happens…" Becky pauses.

"What?" asked John. "If what happens?"

Becky continues. "If something happens, like a sickness or death. You can't come back."

#9 Timing is everything

"Heads up." Says Jennifer from her desktop. John turns to see the familiar face of Angela approaching from behind.

"John, we have to talk."

"Good to see you too Ange. Please, let's talk in my office."
Becky, Patrick, Mike and Jennifer have seen this look before, do
not say a word and continue their work. John and Angela head up
the stairs to his office, Becky thinks *Captain and Tannille* but does
not feel like laughing this time. John shuts the door behind them
and sees Christine in a small window on his screen, just where he
left her.

Back on the floor, Becky turns to Patrick, "Did you see what he
did with my water?"

"Yeah, I thought I was going to fall off my chair, how did he do
that?"

"I don't know," replies Becky. "I hope I didn't look like I was
freaked out. I thought stuff like that was only for certain … you
know … certain folks."

"Don't look at me like that Becky," replies Patrick.

Angela takes a seat next to John, crosses her legs properly and
pleasantly begins, "I see you have made the most of your time thus
far and have taken the opportunity to get acquainted with your
staff."

"Yes, thanks." John replies. "They are a great group of kids. I think we will be able to make some progress, no, I know we will make some progress."

"Now the real deal John", Angela continues, "before your arrival, the Chairman was ready to pull the plug on our project."

"Pull the plug?" says John.

"Yes," Angela adds, "pull the plug…fire and brimstone, tidal waves … Hollywood would be proud."

"Well," John questions, "what happened, that seems a bit extreme if you ask me, why the change of heart?"

Angela continues, "You see, it is not that the Chairman wants to pull the plug, he has quite the investment here but there is a chance we could lose control of the entire project.

"What, like a hostile takeover." Inquires John.

"Well, in a way, you see good has prevailed over evil since the beginning and thus we have maintained control. However, the balance is getting dangerously close to being in favor of evil and if that happens, the hostile takeover will be complete. If that happens, the project will spiral to the depths, taking all with it. The chairman will not allow the good that is left to suffer with this fate. I have convinced The Chairman to give you a shot, a shot at turning things around. You don't have to save the world John, you just need to provide an up-tick. In a way, you were born for this job."

#10 God save the Queen

Angels come to earth to rescue a fallen child. Man can do the same

Angels whisper love to the ears of the deaf. Singing out their name.

Angels will sing for faith to rise up, the world can listen to the harmony

Angels will return to the heavens above, someday we hope to accompany

Angela is done, she has left to go where she goes, John does not know or care where she goes or what she does when she gets there. He is left alone in his new home sitting at a new desk with a new task, staring at an old love that never happened. Christine is on Earth, she is also alone. She is sitting at her kitchen table with one light on in an otherwise dark apartment. Like anyone, Christine has work to do, she has a new reading program to administer. On the kitchen table is a large plastic bin full of handouts and folders. The folders contain manuals and the manuals contain instructions.

This program is more difficult than the last, the content is tougher and Christine is not nearly as motivated as she used to be. As she looks at the daunting task on the table where she sits in the center of her mid size kitchen, Christine refocuses her vision to the blurred picture fixed to the almond refrigerator in the background of her sight line.

Christmas 2006, is the tagline bordering the lower portion of the picture. Pictured just above is Christine's mom and dad. Her dad is behind her mom with his arms around her waist, tan foreheads and big smiles. Christine recalls how nervous her mom was before this trip. Dad's surprises were surprises all right. That doesn't mean they are all good, just surprising, she was there when her dad surprised mom with a seven day Caribbean cruise.

She knows her mother so well, when the tickets were opened, Christine remembers clenching her teeth and holding her breadth awaiting mom's response to what she used to tell Christine was a "seven day sentence as sea." Like usual, mom was very graceful, smiled and gave dad a big hug and a kiss. They had fun, not because of the cruise but because they were together. Their love is so strong you can almost feel it from the picture.

She remembers how fun it was taking their Christmas picture every year. It was a different place every time. Not some exotic locale or anything, well … sometimes. Just different, fun places, either lying in the snow under an evergreen or next to the tree in the town square.

Christine misses that, they don't do that anymore, life has moved on. She sits in the quiet, one light on apartment and tries to concentrate but misses a man she never knew. She loves her students and her family and will rely on that love tonight.

John quietly stands up and walks into the hall overlooking the Central Command work stations where his lead team is doing their monitoring. In unison they all turn their heads to look towards John. John raises one hand and gestures for them to come to him. He turns to return to his office as the four rise and make way. One by one, Becky, Patrick, Mike and Jennifer file into Johns office and one by one take a place next to each other in front of John's desk.

John, with elbows on arms of chair and fingers crossed begins, "How is everybody feeling? Does anyone need a break, a nap or anything? What are our hours? When do we sleep? We are going to get busy and I want to make sure everyone is up to task."

"We don't sleep." Says Mike.

"Nope, don't need it." Remarks Patrick.

"We do eat though." Adds Jennifer.

John looks at Becky. "Well, aren't you going to add anything?

"I like pizza." Becky says with a smile.

"Thanks Donatello, but we need to do something." John explains his conversation with Angela to the now enlightened crowd and continues, "Where is that damned rulebook? Is there a damned rulebook? We are going to have to can the book," Jennifer lets out a short gasp and John pauses momentarily, "no… not that Book, our book, the rule book. If I've experienced anything, it's that anyone who follows the so called rules will never leave the middle of the pack. It is time we move to the front. "I'm going." says John.

"What do you mean" cries Becky, "you can't quit now. We need your help, we have got to do something … OK, whatever, fine we don't need you we can do this ourselves. This is great, we are all screwed, wrap it up folks let's hit the showers.

John chimes in, "Wow, nice job on whipping through those 12 steps Becks. That is not what I mean, I mean I'm going in, I need you to monitor me, I am going to talk to Christine."

"What?' says Mike, "How long have you even known this women? You are going to risk everything, including your own eternity?"

"Please, John adds, "we are going with this? Trust me." These words from John are not a question but a statement. True, John has spent more time daydreaming about Christine than actually spending physical time. He knows her. The time they have spent together was real, as real as the 20th year, as real as John's final moment on Earth.

John tries to explain, "I don't know how often people spend real time with one another, there is always such … guardedness, if that is even a word. Someplace down the line people have forgotten how to be themselves, so worried about what others think or perceive. Not trusting in themselves … you know? If I've learned anything over the years it's that you have to believe in yourself, knowing you're not always going to be right but willing to make mistakes and move on, otherwise all your doing is treading water.

All I know is with that first moment I could see within her soul. I could see the truth in her smile." John knows this to be true for when they spoke it was from the heart and nothing was pretend. He loved her like a father and a lover without ever touching her. Loved her because of who she is, not something she did or said, wanted to be or was.

#11 A wink in time

There is a pause, and then John speaks. "But … before I go, I need to know you guys. You all seem so young and about the same age. We are going to get in some shit together here, pardon my French and before that happens I have a couple questions, let's start with you Jen. How did you get here?

July 1987 – Madison, Wisconsin

Jennifer lies on her bed and rubs her eyes for what seems like an hour, her red, oversized Badger shirt and pink pajamas complement the pink fuzzy slippers well. It's 7am and she does not want to get out of bed. The transition is tough, her senior year classes started after 10am for a reason. It is time however, the alarm has gone off and good old Stevie Winwood is singing about a higher love.

"A higher love indeed." Jennifer says to herself. Her closet is full of jeans and t-shirts making the decision and easy one. Good thing is, being an intern at the local radio station was an informal gig. This makes Jennifer's decision to major in broadcasting an even sweeter one.

"Jenny! You up?" travels up the stairs, down the hall and comes to a rest upon Jennifer's double pierced ears.

"Yeah dad, be right down!"

Jennifer can smell breakfast and hear CBS news as she makes her way to the family kitchen.

"Oh, c'mon Ollie, tell the truth."

"Dad, stop talking to the TV please, it is so disturbing."

"This is important stuff Jenny. You're an adult now, you should be paying attention to this. I made you some pancakes, want some coffee or juice?"

"One pancake please, only one and not that giant sized thing you make that covers the entire plate. It gives me a stomach ache."

Jennifer's dad complies, just as he always has. Anything for my little girl, he would always say.

"Where's mom?"

"She had an early showing today. She left about a half hour ago."

"I should get going too, thanks for breakfast pops."

"No problem, have fun at work today Jenny."

Jennifer's parents bought her a cute, gently used white '81 mustang for a graduation present. She wasn't too hip on the red interior, but was grateful anyway and wondered why they made it … in her own words "so utterly red."

"You are listening to Madison's fave of fave's." The voice over the car stereo howl's in excitement, surely having the desired effect on all two hundred and fifty one listeners this morning. The favorites of the favorites moniker was Randy, Jennifer's new boss' idea. He started radio life as an intern as well and Jennifer is quite fond of him. She is almost certain the attraction is mutual.

The tinny radio voice is Charlie Watts, "Don't go away folks, award winning Steve Winwood coming your way, time to pay the bills, be back in 60 seconds on Madison's 105.1, the fave of fave's." Charlie Watts began life as Charles Wicker, known mostly as "Chuck the Wacky" by his school mates.

"I'd rather stick a sharp object in my eye, sorry Chuckles."
Jennifer mumbles to herself as she turns the large plastic volume
knob to low, then "click" to off. Jennifer is dedicated but not that
dedicated.

When Jennifer made her choice on jeans it was not the typical
random grab from the clean jeans stack in her closet. These are **her**
fave of faves, her best fitting, complimentary, curve hugging,
special occasion jeans. She knows she looks good in these bad
boys and thinks … no … hopes Randy with think so as well.

Jennifer is the kind of girl boys are afraid to approach so they
watch from a distance, watching and talking amongst themselves,
nerves twitching, like two sticks trying to light a fire of courage.
What if they may say the wrong thing prompting the pretty blonde
to laugh and laugh, forever damning the poor boy to a life of
loneliness and misery.

Randy is not afraid, he is confident and successful. He's the
manager of a radio station, big time stuff indeed. He is also older,
and with that, Jennifer is no daunting figure.

Randy opens the small office door where Jennifer makes her sales calls and leans in, "Hey Jenny, what'cha doing after hours later?'

Jenny looks up from her list and smiles, "Today? I don't think I have anything going later, why do you ask?"

Randy is now leaning up against the door keeping it open with his left shoulder, right hand in pocket, too cool for school. "Buddy of mine is having a get together, small shindig, nothing big. You in?"

"Sure, sounds fun, what time?"

"Eight'ish, you know the mattress factory they turned into apartments? You know, down by the river, across from where Joe's dockside eatery was?"

"Yeah, I haven't been by there since I've been back home, but I'll find it."

"Great" says Randy coolly and points in Jennifer's direction. "Apartment 3G, see ya there."

Jennifer returns to her open closet for a quick change before heading up the short distance on highway 51. Only the top requires a change, no need to change the jeans, not these jeans. With one hanger in hand and decisiveness out of mind, Jennifer's phone line begins ringing. Dad was kind enough to get Jennifer her own line when she agreed to come live at home, "It will give you a little time to get your feet firmly planted into adult life," he said.

Jennifer routinely flips one single hanger to the other hand and quickly answers her phone. "Hello, hey Michelle, what's up? Tonight? Can't tonight, Randy asked me out! Can you believe it? I am going to meet him at the Riverside apartments, isn't that awesome! Yes, by myself, I'll be fine, Randy's a great guy. I'll be careful, thanks for caring, love you. I will call you first thing! Wish me luck. Chow."

As Jennifer pulls into the vast parking lot of the Riverside apartment complex she thinks to herself, "little shindig, geez, this place is packed." It is not difficult to find apartment 3G today, there is music and a stream of energized party zombies spawning to and from the double glass door entrance of this massive complex. The spawning continues up the stairs, three flights to the top floor, G apartment is the source of the rhythm, top floor, to the right.

Jennifer is used to this sort of controlled mayhem, been doing it for four years now. This is different somehow; Jennifer's nervous system sends a shot across the bow. What is it, she thinks but continues upward, toward the source, the rhythmic call of the wild. It's the faces, she thinks to herself, the innocent, youthful faces back at the University are gone, replaced by older more determined, hardened party goers.

Still, Jennifer is here to see Randy and continues on, she has a destination. At the top to the right, Jennifer enters apartment 3G, there is Randy, sitting on the counter in the kitchen, drink in hand. He sees Jennifer, smacks his buddy in the chest and points in her direction.

The entrance to the apartment leads into the living area of considerable size for an apartment, there is a large window type pass through from the living room to the kitchen, on this pass through is a counter loaded with liquors and paraphernalia of every type, many of which Jennifer does not recognize. Through this window opening between the kitchen and living room, Randy motions to Jennifer to join him in the kitchen.

This sounds easier than it is, the way must be navigated, as Jennifer navigates her way, Randy again hits is buddy in the chest and points … not to Jennifer this time but to a drink he has readied on the bar.

Jennifer is excited to make it to the kitchen, things already seem a bit hazy in this place. The loud music, fluorescent lighting and smoke from the group chaining at the dinette table make this a scene from a sick and twisted Sesame Street episode of "which one of these does not belong".

The voice in Jennifer's head is screaming "about face!" She doesn't hear it, what she does do is reach out and take the drink from Randy's pathetic, unjust hand.

"Then what happened?" John queries.

Jennifer looks at John and then to the others. There is no shame in this place, it is understood by all the sins and selections, good and bad are behind us now. "I was scared but I took it, I passed out and never woke up. When Angela brought me here, everyone was great and I have been here since."

John makes a mental note of the matter of fact nature of Jennifer's story, a beautiful young girl taken in the prime of her life, leaving behind a family and friends. It shouldn't have to be that way. "Thanks Jen," John remarked, "How bout you Mike?"

April 1995 – Philadelphia, Pennsylvania

"You excited Mikey?

"Yeah Mom, I'm excited." Replies Mike.

"Graduation is only two months away. I am keeping an eye out for something from Rowan. I promise I won't open anything, OK? Have a good day, will you be home for dinner?"

"Yeah, thanks."

Mike is excited, excited to be moving on. High school is not what he expected, he hopes college will be different. Rowan University in South Jersey is just the ticket for Mike. It is just far enough but not too far from a place where Mike has few friends and fewer fond memories.

Back in grade school and junior high things were different. Mike doesn't remember having to try so hard to fit in, it just sort of happened.

Here, in this high school, Mikes' two buddies, Eddie and Shaun are it. Neither Eddie nor Shaun are in Mike's lunch period this semester, which sucks for Mike.

The dull faced, not so happy to be here lunch line cashier shows Mike the palm of her hand, "That will be seventy five cents."

Mike hands over three quarters, takes his plastic apple juice container and looks around the crowded lunch room. He knows these kids, well over one hundred kids in this lunchroom and he knows most of them. Over a hundred kids at twelve foot tables with twelve foot benches attached, spreading out lunch bags and slapping down trays of food.

The problem is, he can't each lunch with them. Sure, no one is stopping him from grabbing an available position and wolfing down his lunch, no one but himself that is.

There is a feeling of un-acceptance that is undeniable, he doesn't belong to any of these groups and any of these tables and he knows it. It would be so obvious if Mike tried to take a place at one of these tables, so very obvious that he does not belong.

Mike heads to his usual spot this lunch period, a quaint little lunch spot under the stairs in the Northeast stairwell. From this vantage point Mike has a clear view of the road in front of the school. As each car passes, Mike's wish is that he was a passenger, with whomever, going wherever.

The sweet shrill of the afternoon bell sends Mike and a sea of sockless boat shoes recklessly into the school parking lot. Just past the row of yellow gleaming buses, Mike catches up with Eddie.

"Dude, hey, Eddie! We going to the game tonight"

Eddie contorts his face and cocks his head to one side before blurting out. "Does a bear shit in the woods? Huh, does it Mack daddy?"

Mike looks at Eddie and laughs. "First pitch is seven thirty five, don't be late. I'm eating dinner first, my mom wants me home for that, but I'll see you at the game."

"Smell ya' later" confirms Eddie.

Mike scrapes the bottom of his dinner plate with his fork and proclaims, "Good stuff maw, once again I maintain my standing as a charter member of the clean your plate club." After a short pause, "you know me and Eddie are going to Veterans to see the Phillies tonight right? You remember, I got the tickets from Uncle Ralphie? Fregosi's got Shilling starting tonight."

"I remember … make sure you bring a jacket, I know it's nice out right now, but you know how it is. Once that sun goes down, the temp is going with it. Say high to Eddie for me."

Curt Shilling wins tonight and goes seven and five for the year. Eddie and Mike high five and head to the exits, the wind is picking up and the rain is starting to come down pretty steady now.

As the boys run to Mike's car and hurriedly jump in the front seats, they laugh and splash the entire way. Mike thinks of all the things he is running from, Eddie is not one of them; he will miss him when school is over, but will remember him well.

"I always thought Shilling looked best in a Phillies uniform," says John, now sitting on the front of his desk, arms crossed.

"Me too," says Mike. "Anyway, I was driving this guy Eddie home when it happened. This drunk dude went through an intersection, that's when I met Angela…she thought I would fit in here."

"I can relate" says John. "Thanks Mike."

"Pat? You willing to jump in?" asks John.

July 4th 1975 – Billings, Montana

"Why is everything so far from everything?" Shannon looks at Patrick with a perplexed expression sprinkled with a dash of disbelief.

Patrick and Shannon shadow the river up I-94 towards Forsyth.

"You get used to it, when you get in the car you know you gotta go a half hour minimum to get anywhere." Patrick has both hands on the top quarter of the steering wheel and a grin on his face. This grin is a constant, some folks think it's insanity but to those in the know … well … some people are just content.

Cruisin' along I-94 on a hot summer day, windows down, with a friend on the way to see friends, what is there not to grin about? A person can see a great distance in any direction in a landscape such as this. As far as the eye can see some say, not true say I. The eye can see farther than you think, it is the road ahead that chooses to hide that which lies beyond the horizon.

During their sophomore year in college, Patrick and Shannon have become good friends. When Shannon was dating Tom, Patrick's roommate freshman year, Patrick's call of duty was to walk Shannon home when Tom would eventually and systematically drink himself to sleep. It was only a fifteen minute jaunt through the quad, but still, nothing good happens after two a.m.

The road Patrick and Shannon currently navigate leads to Tom's place. Everyone has remained good friends, a two month dating cycle in college is but a casual introduction. Shannon is the only out of towner and Patrick was more than willing to make the drive and escort Shannon once again through the wilderness.

"This'll be fun," Patrick takes a quick glance Shannon's way and then back to the road, they're clipping along pretty good and Patrick's old jalopy requires a certain amount of attention. "Tom's old man has this ranch in the boonies, he said he throws this party every year."

Shannon looks at Patrick with a "you think?" expression so detailed that it requires no words.

"I know, you don't have to say, the boonies, this whole place is the boonies, right?" He continues. "Every fourth, Tom buries a pig, gets a ton of fireworks and has the biggest bonfire north of Texas."

"Why would anyone want to bury a pig?" asks Shannon, now serving up a side of disgust.

"Well, not just burying a pig, barbecuing a pig. Tom said you dig a hole and bury the pig with coals to cook it. It's sounds awesome." Patrick looks at Shannon, again … quickly to Shannon and back to the passing pavement. "I take it we'll stop at circle K at the next exit?"

"Yeah huh." Shannon fully agrees.

"Holy crap." Shannon remarks as she exits the car, circle K bag in hand. "Look at all these people."

"There must be a hundred cars?" Patrick joins Shannon just off the stairs to the porch leading into Tom's place. "Remind me later, I have a Cubs cap in the car for you. Tom said the fireworks got so crazy one year a bottle rocket caught a girls' hair on fire."

"Remind you later? Remind me later … the Cubs? Patrick and Shannon pause on the porch at the top of the steps. They both turn to survey the sea of cars and the approaching sunset.

"Dude! You made it!" Tom kicks open the screen door, it snaps back just as suddenly as it was kicked open. The wooden frame whacks Tom in the forehead and he stumbles back into the darkness.

Patrick and Shannon look at each other and laugh.

"Dude, you're just in time." Tom recovers quickly and tries again, this time using the preferred method. "It's bottle rocket bingo time!" Tom puts his right arm around Patrick's shoulder and leads him back down the front steps.

Patrick does not object, he is here for a good time, bottle rocket bingo sounds fun. He doesn't know what it is but that is not important, Patrick is young and invincible.

"Hey, grab that six pack and pack of rockets, where'd you park that heap at?" Tom inquires.

Without question Patrick grabs a six pack and rockets then points in the direction of his car. "Shotgun." He says. Patrick is an adventurous young soul and adventure waits.

Tom cups his hands around his mouth as if howling at the moon, "Game on!" he yells.

Shannon looks on as four pairs of equally adventurous lads run to their cars and speed into the adjoining field. Over the next hour they drive, laugh and shoot bottle rockets at each other through the windows of speeding cars. The hour ends abruptly as Tom runs Patrick's car into a Ponderosa Pine.

Patrick and Tom converge to assess the damage to the front of the vehicle. With hands on hips and a good buzz on, Patrick looks to Tom and back to his now v-shaped bumper. "Let's get some pig!"

Too far to walk, the pair drive Patrick's damaged auto into the heart of the party, through hoards of partiers banging on the hood and roof of the car. They slowly drive through the crowd in an attempt to get as close to the barbecue as possible. Now it's complete anarchy, bottle rockets and fireworks of every imaginable kind whiz by and explode from all directions.

Patrick watches in amazement as some deranged reveler runs by him with the pigs' head held high in triumph. To his further amazement, this same reveler plants the head on Patrick's bumper, replacing the hood ornament left under the Pine tree. Now, almost surreal, will this scene never end, the same guy puts an object with a long wick in the pigs' mouth, lights it and runs yelling like a monkey. Patrick closes his eyes and turns away before the explosion.

Patrick looks at Tom, "Looks like I'm spending the night."

"Sor'right." Tom replies, "It's almost midnight. We have a tradition here, midnight on the fourth, me and my high school buddies, you know, our bottle rocket bingo combatants, well …

meet on the roof and pass a bottle of Stoly. You're in buddy, c'mon, I'll show you.

Tom's house is a small single story L-shaped ranch, to the south is a three sided, triangular shaped antennae tower reaching close to fifty feet into the sky. A combo TV and radio antennae, the placement is just outside the living room window to feed the cable out the window, up the center of the tower and to the antennae.

Shannon called it an evening long ago and sees the gathering through the window from her chair in the living. She gets up and crouches to see what is going on. "What's up guys?" she says. "Don't even tell me you're going up that."

Patrick looks up. He hears the same sentence in his head, not from Shannon's voice but another. He can't hear Shannon through the window although she is only a few feet away, the anarchy outside has not burned itself out yet and drowns out Shannon's protest.

Patrick steps up to the tower and gives it a shake. It's a bit rusty but firmly established on a good sized concrete slab. No time like the present and begins his ascent.

John is amazed at this story but remains seated at the front of his desk, hands now at his sides cupped around the front edges of the desk.

Patrick continues his story, "This thing was like fifty feet tall, I was supposed to get off at the roof height which was only fifteen feet high or so, but no ... I decided to go all the way to the top. I fell ... no soft landing for me. Happy 4th everyone. Then, like these other cats, Angela brought me here."

"Dude." Replies John, "Raw deal."

"OK." Says John, "Thanks for sharing. I'm sorry for everything ... but I'm glad to have met you and glad you've got my back."

"Ahem" Becky interrupts. "Don't you want ... "

John interrupts back. "No Becks, that's OK, I understand if you don't want to talk about it."

Becky is firm and continues. "I'm good...and I remember everything as well.

Summer 1939, New York, New York

A thousand gallons of sweat rain down where the ashes once called home. A crowd of two hundred thousand makes their way through Flushing Meadow Park, wide eyed and amazed. Adult men and women looking and pointing like kids at their first trip to the circus with a seat in the center ring.

"There! There's the capsule." Becky's dad, Harvey, points to a ninety inch long capsule glimmering in the summer sun. "Five thousand years Joan, look at that, no one will see that again for five thousand years. Isn't that amazing?"

Joan is happy for Harvey, he is smiling. He has looked forward to this day for months. The odd jobs have the family of six surviving another day, every hour of every day that passes leads to better times. They have to.

Joan can't tell him, not yet. Smiles don't come around very often these days. They will have an argument soon enough, she will tell him then.

Harvey and Joan walk arm in arm passed the great works of DaVinci and Michelangelo, the great waterfall and the parachute jump. They exist in a world of great promise; they can see it right before their eyes. This promise gives strength, as it is intended to do, to make it through the next hour of the next day, leading to better times. It has to.

Back home a small, colorless apartment remains quiet. Harvey and Joan's three boys sleep the afternoon away. A full mattress rests on the dusty wood floor, side by side they sleep. Their only daughter, the youngest of the four naps on grandma's lap, the smooth, melodic voices of Parks Johnson and Wally Butterworth emanate from the single speaker radio residing on the table next to Grandma's good ear.

She can't tell him, she won't ... not yet that is. Harvey has done everything possible to make sure the babies are fed. The lines, the handouts ... even though they don't talk much anymore she knows it's taking a toll on her husband. Joan sits quietly on the concrete steps of their four story apartment building in South Queens. She doesn't know it but the twitching has begun. Joan sits hunched over with her elbows between her legs, hands ringing and head twitching. Joan is twelve weeks pregnant, Becky grows strong inside her mother, she is not alone. As Becky grows in her mother's womb, a demon grows in her mother's soul.

Harvey and grandma noticed the erratic behavior and mildly violent mood swings but do not speak of it. Grandma over compensates with the boys and the baby is too young to notice. Harvey is working three jobs that span the twenty four hours we are allotted each day. He sleeps when he can and works when allowed.

When Joan began spending the days in bed, grandma felt a bittersweet relief. She cried for her daughter most nights, the time of the day when the children are asleep and the night is quiet with the exception of your thoughts. Joan cried as well, from her bed she would twitch and cry out as she rolled back and forth clutching her belly. The times when she did eat and bathe, which was not often, she would do so in the middle of the night.

That Fall, on a cool dry night, Joan bypassed the small kitchen and exited the apartment barefoot into the streets. Breathing heavy and near exhaustion Joan comes to a stop at the base of the apartment steps that lead to the sidewalk. She requires a pause, one hand on the wrought iron rail and the other holding her small protruding belly. Joan is panting heavily, the breathing echoes like a forest fire in Joan's head. Over the roaring in her head is another sound, a voice in the distance, soft and calming. Joan begins to relax and breathe a bit easier. The hand cupping Becky reaches for the steps as Joan prepares to sit. The steps are cool and dry in respect for the night air. Joan lies back on the steps and rests her head on the straw weave welcome mat.

Becky is born in the rare silence on a South Queens sidewalk. The twitching has stopped and Joan is able to walk calmly across the street, not far from where they picked up the number seven train to Flushing Meadow Park a few months ago.

Becky never takes her eyes from John and John never takes his eyes from Becky. John does not comment or speak as Becky tells her tale.

"It was cold… so it didn't take long. I remember the cover of the trash can, rusty, grey metal, when it opened up, there was Angela. She carefully reached in and lifted me out. She was very warm and I was never scared. When you come here as a baby or a child, you grow up in Heaven, its' beautiful there. I am the only one in this place that has been there. I would do anything for Angela and this project … that is why I am here."

"Becks, thanks, you're the best. You guys have my back, right?" John looks into the eyes of his new best friends, "Guys, sorry. I really don't know why, I feel kinda stupid. I wish I had a speech, some words of wisdom…something. I'm scared, anxious, excited…don't rightly know. The thing is, please be patient cuz I'm talking and thinking at the same time." John raises his hands to his shoulders in defense of his words. "I really don't know if I'm going back to save the world or to say goodbye to Christine. All of you have unfinished business. All of you deserve to say goodbye…or" John pauses to look Becky's way. "To at least ask why? I'll understand if I'm on my own. I just want to be open with everyone here. I want all of you to understand what is in my heart." John takes a moment and ponders. "It's funny, I've never felt this way before. There are no barriers between us whatsoever. I love you guys." John thinks of Christine. He realizes she has not for a moment left his consciousness. The love for his new friends creates a longing for Christine that challenges the pain of all that have suffered before him.

Without hesitation, John heads for the door, the door he entered from a foggy parking lot what seems like a hundred lifetimes ago. A door he cannot shut, for it will be shut for him.

#12 A rose by any other name

I smell funny. Not a good funny either, a funky funny. John wakes up in an alley

around the corner from Christine's apartment. The sun is shining and the concrete is warm, this is good. His bones ache and it takes several minutes to stand. The brick wall of the alley building is rough and the mortar crumbles under John's hand as he uses the wall for support, pieces of it sticking to John's clothes as well as his skin. The texture feels like home and is strangely pleasant. John begins the short journey to exit his new found alley home and enter the sidewalk adjacent. As he passes a broken window, through the dirt and oily glaze John sees his new self. He is old, years of wrinkles like rings of a tree count the decades on this face.

Is this me? John thinks to himself as he gently touches his face with his hands. Is this me when I am old or someone else altogether? Before John can come to a conclusion, a cold hand of stone comes down hard on his shoulder.

"You gotta love the smell of an alley in the afternoon, the freshly emptied dumpster, the rotting rats and even rottener fish. But my personal favorite is the steamy sewer gas creeping out of the ground like a drunken sailor's morning breath. What do you think, eh… John?"

John is silent and unmoved. The man with the less than gracious greeting is still directly behind him with the strength of a thousand men on his shoulder. In the window where John greeted his new and now dangerously vulnerable image is not only himself, but a tall man in a black hat with the rim pulled down. He does not need to look down for confirmation, for he knows what he will see, black boots … black boots carrying a faceless man.

"I am not who you think I am." John is surprised by the weakness of his voice. If he heard this voice from the other side of the table, surely this much effort to speak in such a soft voice must be painful. But it was not, it was as it should be.

"Oh John!" The faceless man exclaims. "Now I am hurt, you have pained me deeply. After all we have been through together, why … you don't remember me?"

The faceless man removes the hand from John's shoulder. This relief is immeasurable. Although John remains still, the man in the black hat and boots begins to pace back and forth. With each step the crackle of old bones and brick mortar crunch under the boots of this faceless, each step is heard loud and clear causing John to cringe and grit his teeth.

In a place, far, far away … a band of four begins to play. Four people from four places, four people committed to each other by love and respect. Four people that would have and could have never met on a planet called Earth in a time that does not exist. But here they are, four people looking at a screen in a faraway place, at a place they could have been friends forever. A place they could have shared their lives, could have laughed and cried and rejoiced in that ever fleeting moment.

They are next to each other at two stations. Becky and Patrick at one … Mike and Jennifer at the other. Becky and Patrick are monitoring John and the others … well, they have work to do.

"Please, I just wish to be left alone, I have no quarrel with you, I don't know who you are." John explains to the faceless man.

With this, the man stops and leans in closely to Johns ear. With a

wink and a whisper, the man offers this explanation.

"Then let me remind you my dear man, you remember me, your

old pal Max. It's good to see you again."

John turns to Max to confront his pursuer, the black brim of his

hat and coat collar steam with the calmness of the morning dew.

John tries to concentrate, to gain clarity beyond the steaming

collar, the face is but a blur and no amount of correction will help.

"Fine," John attempts to be firm. "But a brief encounter in a

parking lot does not constitute a history. I turned down your offer

and I will be on my way."

With this remark, Maxwell let's out a thunderous laugh. "Oh

John!" Maxwell remarks "You could always make me laugh."

John remains firm but is growing uneasy. He is not sure the pit in

his stomach is his new body or something else, something far more

ominous.

"That?" Maxwell continues. "That is not what I am talking

about. Our history is much more than that. All of a sudden I am

not your buddy anymore? Now that you're a goody two shoes.

Well, John, then I'm Ralph Edwards and this is your life! Brought to you by some product that will make you shit! Where should I start, how about that little tart on Murphy's hill. Took advantage of that didn't you? How about all those fine little trinkets you helped yourself to around the Holidays. Yeah, you were just a kid, but you were just getting started. The cheating in school, the lying, you were my buddy back then weren't you? Who was there for you when you got your fist break Johnny boy? It was me John, your old pal Maxwell."

John did not like hearing those words, in fact, he hated hearing those words, for they quickly became all too familiar. Truth should not be your enemy. Your old pal Maxwell … he had heard those words before. Wasn't there this crazy kid he hung around with in grade school? Or maybe Jr. High?

"I made things right, Max." John chimed in. "I said I was sorry and I made things right." John whispered to himself, not quite sure why he knows this as fact. "I never said I was perfect! John screamed, staring into the vast wasteland of Max's identity. "I was ready to accept my punishment, whatever it was and did not ask for this!"

"It is not about asking for something, John." Max is more resolute than before. "Asking for forgiveness is like pissing up a flagpole. Sure, it will pass the time and relieve the ache in your kidneys but it won't get you up the pole or raise the flag for that matter. You had to go and be good. You had to go and let decency, nonjudgmental thought and caring rule your world. You went and helped people, gave to the poor and all that non-sense." Then Max's voice became softer and almost sad, "You had to go off and really love people. As the story goes you looked up at the sky one day and felt peace and love. You had to go and sacrifice it all, didn't you? You turned your back on me John."

With that, Max was angry again, as his voice rose, he seemed to gain size and grow ever darker. "With that you will pay, we will be together again John, you will work for me!" Max raised his hand, John could see the brick in his hand, the blue sky and soft clouds in the background. Max begins to lower the brick, the one that not too long ago felt calming to the touch.

An eerily, soft "thud" as Max hits the pavement. John, with eyes clenched in anticipation of the blow slowly opens his old, weary eyes. Christine is there, shaking and crying. She had never hurt another human being in her life but could not let this thug hurt this poor, defenseless old man. The sheer recklessness of her actions gives way to anxiety forcing Christine to ramble; her Mom always teased Christine about her rambling when she was nervous.

"Oh my God," she says, "I am so sorry, I was grading papers, then got hungry and decided to make a snack instead of go out … then I got this wicked craving for a pumpkin spice latte."

At this statement, somewhere, far, far away, a band of four is high-fiving.

"Then I saw that guy giving you a hard time … that is just wrong, the big jerk … you poor thing."

Fortunately for Christine, this alley was like many others in this city, in need of some housekeeping. With far too little time to spare, only moments before Max was to strike John, Christine grabbed a nearby garbage can lid and felled Maxwell with one blow.

#13 Home is never how you left it

John leans against the brick that almost betrayed him and slides to a seat on the still warm pavement. Christine kneels next to the gentleman only to see a familiarity in his eyes.

"Are you ok?" She asks. John does not speak, if he does that will mean this moment has fleeted, an aforementioned moment in time that defines our existence. In John's mind the question of "are you ok" is meant for him. In his mind John is grabbing Christine by both arms and explaining it all, "Yes, yes I'm ok, thanks for caring, you must care, you have to because I care about you! That is why you are asking if I'm ok. Let's not let this little dying thing get between us." Such words are not spoken, John is silent.

It is not John holding Christine by both arms but Christine that tenderly grasps John's arms. "Can you hear me?" Christine asks, "If you can, nod your head." As Christine nods her head in example, Johns begins to speak.

"I can hear, I can hear you fine, thank you."

John's eyes panic. Desperate to remain fixed into Christine's deep … wonderful eyes that reveal and reduce John to his core. He is no longer a man, set on this Earth to divide and conquer, just a spectator, resolved to swim in the glory of this absolute.

The eyes that panic also betray, for John, Christine is a blink in a sand storm. He has not the luxury of history or the possibility of a future with Christine. Today, John's eyes must take in everything,

every angle of Christine's nose, the sweeping beauty of her lips …
the gentle crest of her cheeks and the rise and fall of her hair. John
closes his eyes in an attempt to burn the image for eternal review.
His heart races and he loses concentration, Christine's words
become jumbled. Something so simple, to hold Christine in his
arms, the urge to do so is so monumental it borders catastrophic. In
a bizarre irony that almost angers John in the sense it is not an
intended or a desired emotion, but an emotion that is unavoidable,
completely sub conscious and raw in nature. "Look at you," John
whispers. Not knowing he is speaking. There is such peace in her
eyes. One cannot wage war when one weeps for the glory that
exists in the eyes of their true loves soul. John sees her for the first
time every time. Every time he closes his eyes, every time her
image appears. There is a pause, nothing else exists. It's like slow
motion as John tries to somehow stay connected to earth and
acknowledge the laws of gravity. It is beyond comprehension, for
lack of better words… fucking surreal. John battles with his grip
on reality, is she for real? Is this a dream? He loves her beyond his
own understanding and battles within himself to treat her as a
normal person. She is right? She is a person, she has feelings and

thoughts and regrets like the rest of us, right? For John, she is much more than that.

John cannot express the feelings he has, there is no future here, he is a strange man not only to Christine but to himself. The sensation such as this, wanting it to go away and never wanting it to end is maddening, so utterly maddening he can't stand it but must overcome it as sure as survival requires at least one more … lonely and necessary breadth. There no explanation for an emotion that does not rate on any scale nor can it be dignified by any spoken word. Such is our fate.

Still seated with his back to the wall, John opens his eyes and speaks. "That was a very brave thing you did for me. You put yourself in harms way to help out a stranger. I have done nothing to deserve so much as a glance, let alone such graciousness."

Christine is surprised to hear such speech from a man she assumed was not in control of all capacities. That is what you hear on TV and talk radio, right? That homeless and street people are stricken with a mental disease of some sort or just crazy. To hear coherent speech was not what Christine was expecting, but was pleasantly surprised.

"Why did that man want to hurt you?" As Christine poses this question, she turns to point to the fallen man … surprise number two, Max is gone. She looks back and forth in the alley to be sure of no rebuttal, there is no one around but the pedestrians making their way on the street at the end of the alley. The garbage lid Christine used to repel the giant lies motionless next to a kit kat wrapper and an apple core.

"Our past was in conflict with our future." John explains. "It's complicated." John looks up to Christine, takes a deep breath and maintains his composure. Still seated, one hand on his knee and the other hand L-shaped from chin to cheek on John's unshaven face, remembers he is here for a reason.

"Did you ever think you could make a difference? That by being here, by being born, that there is some reason for that?"

Christine borrows the brick wall and roughly slides to a seat next to John, she has never felt so small and alone as she sits with her arms around her knees in this now shadowy alley. The warmth has faded and a chill is setting in.

From this vantage point, the realization of their surroundings becomes ever more clear and dank. Christine is struggling to understand why this man has just posed the ultimate question. The "why are we here?" question. Looming even larger is the fact that she is OK with this conversation. Mostly, it would be quite unusual for Christine to even walk down an alley, let alone be sitting with a strange man discussing the meaning of life.

"I am sorry, I don't have an answer for you." explains Christine. "I am just a grade school teacher, not a philosopher or some kind of brainiac."

"I see," adds john. "So you **do** make a difference. Can I tell you a story young lady? I would like to hear your commentary upon hearing this tale. May I?"

John stands up with the strength and poise of a much younger man and extends his hand in the direction of the street and the passer byes.

"Would you like to take a walk?"

"Sure," adds Christine, "That is, if you feel up to it."

"I'm good." Replies John, as he begins in the direction of the street. They walk in silence … a good silence, the old fashioned silence of a world without technology. John remembers this comfortable silence as a kid … or maybe a young adult, but that is not all he is remembering. He does recall the silence, the silence of a single man floating in the center of a sea that has not a single ripple created by man.

Christine's blue eyes have been a cloak to the truth Max has uncovered in John's mind cellar, or should we say dungeon. John shakes his head, it's like a vomit of information you can't keep down....won't keep down. Look out brain, I ain't feeling too good.

John and Christine arrive at the mouth of the alley, the street is lively with pedestrians and shoppers alike. The store fronts sit close to the street with multi colored awnings and bright signs with clear explanation to why one should enter. Without hesitation John takes a right, unknowingly heading North on Star Boulevard.

"My name is John, thanks for everything." Christine hesitates for a moment, and then returns to her place alongside John. Her pleasant grin momentarily fades; John knows why and purposely ignores this temporary and nostalgic sadness.

"I have a lesson to teach as well," John continues, "a different sort of lesson than yours to your students of course ... but first, I must preface this story. Just so you know, I am not blaming anyone for my situation, I ... myself and no one else made the choices and my actions were not coerced. As a result, I have not always made the right decisions along the way."

Christine shows concern in those eyes. "What do you mean you blame no one?"

"When I was a younger man, I was not treated well. I do not want to disturb or frighten you so I will not be specific. There was a time, a time when I was much younger that I believe I had a purpose, that I could make a difference. I apologize because it is all too vague. Some time ago I loved and was loved, then it all ended, sort of like a taking a walk in a field of perfect green grass, the sun shining and just enough breeze that it is not to annoying … just right, you know? Then, way too soon, the tide of lush, soft grass ended and a sea of jagged stone began. At this point, I was left to choose a direction without guidance and believe I followed the path of ignorance, greed and self gratification led by a faceless man."

Christine listens without question to this story, her gaze volleys between the street ahead and John's unyielding determination in his face. Somehow Christine understands this story is for the both of them, being told and being heard by this unlikely pair for the first time.

"Somewhere," John continues, "Somewhere down the line I abandoned the path. Not as simple as a fork in the road … no, I had to leave the path and enter the rough in search of another. I believe I did so in hopes that my trail would be harder to find. I learned a lot during that time and eventually discovered a path that was inviting and comfortable. A path with other people on it, good people, for I was completely alone on my previous trail."

"Is that what brought you to the alleyway?" asks Christine. "I am trying to follow you, I have to admit I am a little confused. Was your previous job a bad one, did you loose your job or something?"

"Something like that." John adds. "Actually, I moved into a better position with a better company, doing something to be proud of. But now I feel like I printed out my own diploma from The University of Deception, all dolled up in a golden frame to distract from the fine print."

John stops walking and Christine follows his lead. He looks at Christine for the first time since beginning his tale. The sun is getting lower and is reflecting off a diner window, this causes John to squint and turn his head a bit to look Christine in the eyes. She has never seen a man this full of sorrow and wonders what kind of life this man must have led.

"I really don't deserve anything or anybody.' Johns says softly. "I don't deserve love, I am not sure what love is anymore. I thought … I was strong and had a purpose. I am nothing."

Far, far away, Becky, Patrick, Mike, Jennifer, Angela and all the department heads watch with great interest.

Angela has taken up temporary residence alongside John's staff.

Jennifer looks to Angela. "Hey Angela, something's been bugging me, I can't seem to get my hands around it."

"What is it my dear?" replies Angela

"John's voice, since the first day he arrived … there was something about his voice, a strange familiarity that I can't quite place."

Angela looks at Jennifer, lovingly smiles and places a soft hand on Jennifer's shoulder. "That voice is familiar because it has been your guide all along. The voice in your head, the one that tried to calm you and the one that tried to warn you. The voice that praised you and the voice that punished you. That is why you have heard him before.

#14 Right is right

If you want to understand someone, don't walk a mile in their shoes.

It is not where their shoes are going; it is where their shoes have been.

John turns and slowly begins to return to the alley where this life began, but the brick wall is no longer warm and the sun has been replaced by cold shadows.

"John," Christine calls out. "I have a story too; don't you want to hear it? You know what; I don't care if you want to hear it or not because I'm tellin' it."

John stops and grins ever so slightly. She is a sassy one, he thinks to himself.

"I knew a guy once," Christine continues, "Funny…his name was John, like you. Although we shared but a moment in time," Christine pauses and looks up to the sky … John waits. Christine looks back at John. "He changed my life forever and I will never forget him. I will think of him always …not trying to, I just do, and

I'm going to try John … try to be a better person because of our time together. I can't explain it … the feeling in my heart."

Christine is determined, like John's story, a story of revelation is not only for the audience. "You meet a lot of people in life and there are but a few that can touch you deeply without trying. Like a boy in the woods that carves a symbol in a young tree. The tree and the boy go on without ever crossing paths again, but the symbol remains until the tree falls."

Christine's story is ended but the plea continues. "John, you said you don't know what love is anymore, that you thought you were strong and had a purpose. There must have been a reason you once thought those things. There must have been something or someone in your life that once provided a fuel for your love, strength and purpose. None of us are perfect … we all make mistakes. Remember the reason you once loved and learn from the mistakes you made while walking the wrong path. Remember that reason John, the reason you loved and the strength and purpose will not be far behind. I realize you don't know me and it's not in people's nature, but you have to trust me John. Please trust me."

Christine does not know why she needs this man to believe her. Not just wanting him to believe her but needs him to believe her.

"OK, Christine." John responds. "Now I need you to trust me. These bones are old, would you like to get some coffee?"

"Sure," says Christine. "I know a place right around the corner. They have this Kenyan blend that is to die for."

John gets a pit in his stomach at that last statement. A little close to home. John and Christine walk in silence again. John recalls the time at the airport spent with Christine, just as he has done a thousand times since. She has given him strength again, she has shown him love and it is true, the strength and purpose were not far behind, in fact … they were just sitting there the whole time, waiting for a helping hand to get back in the game.

She is beautiful, no doubt. That is not why he loves her. In his mind he has no clue if she would be protruded as beautiful to others. Doesn't care, either, she could be plain Jane, she could be offensive for that matter. To John she is the most beautiful thing he has ever seen and will feel that way forever.

John and Christine make their way through the gravel parking lot toward the steel steps leading to the entrance of the diner. The night has become cool but the diner is warm and low lit. This gives John some comfort, but with that is a feeling he is being watched, not just watched … more like preyed upon.

The dim interior helps calm him, the vinyl seats are hard, but warm. As John looks around, everything is in its' place. The small, steel rack on the booth top is stocked … ketchup, mustard, tobacco, salt and pepper. The secondary rack is good as well … cream, sugar, blue and yellow packets as well. The gum chewing waitress rounds out this perfect setting. Vera, it says in her oval pin, you must be kidding, he thinks. Christine was on the money and the coffee is as advertised.

John takes a sip and breaks the silence. "I knew this girl one time, we were dating but were great friends the moment we met. I had this little blue truck … a stick shift as I recall. I had this place back then I'd go … great coffee. Anyway, we had just gotten some coffee to go and we were in the truck heading God knows where. Lisa was the girls name; well.. Lisa had taken the lid off to add some sugar and warned me ahead of time to take it easy. Just as she did, I was coming up to a really big bump that was in the parking lot, well actually it was the transition between two parking lots and was a huge dip instead of a bump.." At this point John begins to laugh, the borderline uncontrollable kind, on the edge but still in check. Christine begins to laugh as well, not quite sure but kind of knowing where this might be going.

"Anyhow, I yell, Hold on! And floor it through this huge dip I the parking lot. Hot coffee goes flying everywhere. Lisa looks at me like I am crazy."

At this point John looses it and cannot stop laughing. Now Christine is looking at John like he is crazy as well but cannot help but to laugh along with him.

"Well, Christine asks, "What did she do?"

"That's the thing." Says John, "I started laughing because I did something so utterly and completely stupid … I figured that was it … that our short friendship has come to a quick, but scalding end, then … she started laughing too.

John takes a deep breath that ends in a sigh, "It says a lot about someone when you can keep an open mind and not condemn someone for one miscue of action. Thanks for helping me out back there."

"No problem," Says Christine, "I am glad to have met you."

With another sigh, John wonders how this beautiful woman could find time for coffee with the likes of the man in the alley.

Before John can finish this thought, the waitress politely interrupts, "Excuse me dears." the waitress looks at this unlikely pairing with odd eyes and even stranger expression, "I am sorry to interrupt, but the gentleman at the counter asked me to give this to you. Which one of ya'll is JC?"

The waitress places a large apple pie in the center of the table and offers a standard size white envelope to the pair. John looks at the envelope in the waitress' hand and stretches his neck around the waitress to look down the counter. Besides the steel posted stools and vinyl, the only other visual delights are two women drinking coffee and chain smoking. A few more stools down is a construction worker type reading the paper, the remaining stools remain soulless.

"That'd be me." Replies John. "If you don't mind, could you point out the fellow that passed you this letter and was kind enough to offer some apple pie?"

As the waitress turns, her arm raises in an attempt to point to what is now an empty seat at the end of the counter. "He was there a second ago," she pauses, looks perplexed and slowly begins to mumble as she walks away "better not have stiffed me, for God's sake," the waitress makes her remarks as she sails off to makes her way to the end of the counter.

"JC, huh?" Remarks Christine, "That's cute … and kinda strange you would be getting a letter delivered to you by Little Miss Sunshine. What's up?" Christine asks with a nod.

"Not so sure," replies John. "everything is not always as it seems…and stop grinning at me, my Mom called me JC ok?"

"Ok," confirms Christine. John turns the envelope over a few times; he sees no rush to open prior to a complete inspection. Nothing, just one J followed by a C written in a deep red ink in what looks like an old world calligraphy style.

John turns the envelope and begins to tear it open from the backside, as he does so, Christine let's out a short but undeniable gasp.

"John!" Christine is quite startled and is pointing to the back side of the envelope. "The letters, they're … they're bleeding!"

John looks at Christine and slowly turns the letter over. The lower part of the written letters are running down the paper, over John's finger tips and dripping on the apple pie.

"So they are." He calmly confirms. "So they are." John turns the envelope back over and returns to his task of opening the letter.

"John!" Christine continues. "John! The fricken' envelope is bleeding!"

Fricken', John thinks in his head, she says Fricken', and chuckles momentarily.

"Is this some kind of joke?" Christine is still on edge. "Please fill me in here, I am freaking out little bit. If this is some kind of joke, I don't think it is very funny."

John concentrates deeply on opening this envelope and Christine can see this in his eyes and firm face. She is still in the dark but is calmed by the demeanor of this scruffy old man. She feeds off this and understands it is best to sit and wait, an explanation will come in time. This day has been weird enough and she no longer has a taste for apple pie.

The envelope is opened, Christine watches in silence. John removes the ancient paper with burned edges.

Dear John,

This ain't that kind of Dear John my fine feathered friend. I DO look forward to seeing you and do NOT wish you luck in the future. But I digress. Upon our untimely adjourning of our last meeting I have had time to think. And think I have. I have thought of how vulnerable you are, I have read and re-read the rules. The rules John, you know dem rules. The rules you used to love to break. But seeing as we are old friends, I will give you a chance. Go back! Go back! You will be spared, go back to your hole in the sky. If you don't I will catch you and you can NEVER go back. Say good bye to your pretty friend, I will see to her. You screwed up plenty in the past John, do what's right for a change.

Signed: Your old pal Maxamillion

P.S. Enjoy your pie?

Becky, Patrick, Jennifer & Mike continue to observe, they are now alone together, Angela has other obligations.

"What should we do, Becky?" asks Jennifer. "We have to do something, that Max guy … he is up to something. We can't let anything happen to John, he's our only hope, that … and Christine too."

"I know." Says Becky. "I love you guys, you know that right." Becky looks at all of them, without a word each one of their eyes confirms Becky's question. "Do what you can, keep an eye on us, John is first, remember that."

Without hesitation, Becky heads toward the door. Just like John, the door is closed for her. Mike and Jennifer look to Patrick.

Patrick looks back. "Guys," Patrick says. "Let's keep it together, Becky and John need us right now. You know the drill, monitor and react. Monitor the perimeter around our group and try to keep the peace."

Jennifer and Mike take their seats.

"Got it," says Mike.

"Got it." replies Jennifer.

John folds the letter neatly and returns it to the envelope from which it came. John begins, "My dad had a saying, he said never achieve for the sake of achievement. Set a goal, believe in your goal, work hard with ethics, if you do so, the end product will be achievement. The idea, I guess, is that if you set out just to achieve greatness, you have already failed. That greatness and achievement are the result of hard work and ethics, not greed to be great … or rich for that matter."

"I couldn't argue with that," Says Christine, "Does this have something to do with that envelope?" Christine appears a little shaky.

"Sort of," replies John, "I have something I wish to achieve while I am here, you know … on Earth."

"Uh, yeah John … on earth," says Christine, "It doesn't seem like it today, but that is where we are at. If you know what you wish to achieve, you're ahead of a lot of us … here on earth as you put it. What is it John, I hate to keep asking, but what does it have to do with that bloody envelope!"

"Sorry," John continues, "Just a parlor trick, please don't let that bother you." John looks intently at Christine. " Do you really want to know? You've already helped an old man a great deal, you can go if you wish. I am fine, I thank you for all you've done, and you're a good person with a good heart. You don't need the problems that go with a guy like me."

Christine looks at John and is no longer concerned with the envelope. "Well, my father told me one time," Christine adds, "he said problems are excuses in disguise, you figure it out. All I know is I am concerned. I don't know why, I just am. I want to help you … again … I don't know why … I just do."

"Let's go then." Says John.

"Where?" asks Christine.

"To rid ourselves of any excuse." Replies John as he leads her to the door.

#15 An apple a day

Becky looks up at the star filled sky. She wasn't expecting it to be dark. In reality, she doesn't know what she expected. All she knows is now she is frightened by the darkness. She wasn't expecting to be frightened either. This is all new to Becky, her previous experience here was entirely in darkness but she was never afraid.

"Where am I?" Becky says to herself in a young girls' voice. Becky looks around and then down to her soft, small hands, with her soft small fingers. She turns her hands over for inspection, they are dark. It doesn't take Becky long to determine she has crossed through the door as a young black girl.

In her place, Angela closes her eyes and remembers. She remembers the day Becky became lost. She remembers that day like all the others, for she is the lone savior of all lost children. Angela has no jurisdiction here, Becky is no longer one of her children, no matter how lost she becomes.

Becky's eyes adjust to the surroundings; it is still abnormally dark in the place she lays, about six feet up and to her right two small eyes blaze in the shadows, motionless. Becky has yet to move.

Becky wonders what she is waiting for, for that thing with the eyes to come down, wherever down is and offer her a cup of tea? Why am I just lying here, what am I waiting for. As Becky lays motionless, a single tear rolls down her fresh, cool cheek and pools on the cusp of her tiny ear.

"It's ok mom, I'm fine, don't you worry, I'm a big girl now." Upon speaking those words, Becky sits up, feet flat on the dirty ground, puts her head to her knees and cries.

Two minutes pass, Becky sniffs, wipes her eyes and is ready to face her foe, not knowing she has just defeated her only true enemy.

She stands confidently, wipes the dirt from her lower body and focuses. She is in some sort of stairwell; a grey, grease stained steel door is to her left, a brick wall behind her and on her right side, stairs directly in front of her.

Becky looks to the top of the stairs, "Hey little guy," she says as she slowly makes her way to the city above. Before Becky reaches the top of the stairs, a small grey cat with reflective eyes scurries into the darkness. Becky watches the cat the entire way as she firmly plants both feet on the sidewalk at the top of the stairwell.

"Now what." She says to herself. "Think, think, think." Becky repeats as she taps her tiny fingers to her temples. Becky stands up straight, looks into the darkness and summons up from God knows where, an undeniable determination. "Fate and my friends are with me." Becky says to herself as she heads North into the darkness.

John and Christine navigate the steps exiting the diner, John extends a courteous hand to Christine as they reach the last step.

"It got dark," remarks Christine. "I wonder how late is."

"Hopefully not too late," says John, not referring to the time. John pauses at the bottom of the stairs, Christine without a word pauses with him.

"North." Says John as he points to his right.

"North." Christine confirms. As they walk, in silence again, they unknowingly begin their walk arm in arm. After a short block Christine begins to sing. "Because, because, because, because, because.....because of the wonderful things he does."

Then John joins in. "Where off to see the wizard, the wonderful wizard of Oz."

Up ahead, Becky can hear the laughter of two people apparently enjoying their late night walk about a block behind her. She has reached the street corner and the corner street lamp has illuminated the area quite well. Besides the approaching couple, the streets seem pretty empty in this town.

The sounds of life provide a beacon of comfort even though Becky is very much alone. Becky knows she is alone, but only physically, and that's OK. Loneliness is a complex creature; you don't get there by being physically alone, but mentally alone. Becky knows there are those that are with her, with her now, with her in the past and will be with her until the end. Although Becky has not had the opportunity to experience this in the setting she now inhabits, Patrick, Jennifer and Mike will always be by her side.

Becky has always been fascinated by the stories, the permanence of young love, stories of unforgettable events between young people that last a lifetime, a time that far surpass the actual relationship itself. Life can separate indeed, true love and friendship endures forever.

She is OK with the stories and that she has none of her own. OK with the fact that in the beginning she was a victim. Just as Becky is not alone in the love department, she is not the only victim either. Becky has seen many a wounded heart from her vantage point. She has seen wounded that are determined to heal and the wounded that continue to bleed. Some bleed quietly alone … but some are determined to bleed over others. She's OK with her destiny, her mind is sharp and her determination to stop the bleeding is unwavering.

Becky fondly recalls these stories as she gazes to the stars and feasts on the cool night air. She will never be alone; no one can take her loves away. The singing couple has reached where Becky has escaped to the stars and stop. Like anyone on the planet would do, they look up as well.

"Beautiful night," says Christine.

"Yeah, downright," says Becky as she looks to her new companions. Becky immediately recognizes Christine. "Christine," whispers Becky to herself in a soft voice.

Christine is startled by what she thinks she hears. "Excuse me," says Christine to her new admirer. "Do I know you?"

Becky looks up at the stars again and acts unaware of Christine's query. "Pristine, isn't it, what a pristine night, eh folks?"

Christine lets it go at that, must have been hearing things.

"Yes it is." John joins the conversation. He looks at the young girl and instinctively inquires, "Isn't it kind of late for you to be out? I mean, Ii may not be any of my business but you seem a bit young and a girl and all … to be out here by yourself, especially late at night."

"You're right mister." Replies Becky. "I may have lost my way. I'm new to this place, so to speak, I do believe you could help, if you are so inclined."

"Well my, my," says Christine. "You are quite the polite little thing." With a tip of her head and a slight bow Christine adds. "How may we be of assistance?"

John looks on in amusement with a side order of surrealism.

"My name is Becky, on occasion, Becks for short. Either way is good for me, and you are?"

John quickly intercedes, coincidence … he thinks not but needs to be sure. "John & Christine," he says as he leans in for a closer look. "Becks?" says John with one eye open as if looking through a telescope. "That you?"

"That me John." Says Becky.

"You shouldn't have come here." Says John. "I did not authorize that."

"Authorize?" says Becky. "Sorry, I must have missed that directive at the last meeting." Becky puts one hand on her hip and waves her right index finger in the air, then begins to mimic John's voice as she continues this statement. "If anyone must travel to earth against all known statutes and risk eternal damnation to save my milk toast butt, you will need me to sign this authorization form, thank you." Becky returns to her host child's voice. "Is that the authorization you are referring to?"

John looks at Becky, his eyes raise and his lips press together. "My bad." He says. "Thanks, you're a cute kid." John says with a laugh.

Christine looks on with a wide eyed amazement. She suddenly feels as though it is time to wake up from this dream. As John and Becky go about their exchange they don't notice Christine has become short of breadth and a bit wary. Christine has never fainted in her life but accepts that this is as good a time as any.

"Good night Irene." Says Christine as she stumbles away from John and Becky. John hears this and is quick to Christine's side to stabilize her. John looks around for a place to set Christine down, just to their right is a concrete stoop entering a corner store that inhabits this place. John looks up, the neon sign in the large window reads, Northstar Jewelry and Exchange, funny looking star for a jewelry shop, thinks John, a bit like the Star of David.

John slowly leads Christine to the stoop for a chance to catch her breath and investigate the cause of her ailment. "Christine," asks John, "Are you OK?"

"Jesus," responds Christine, "What is going on here?" Christine is short of breadth and on the verge of hyperventilating but goes on with the line of questioning. "First the letter, now this girl, you know her don't you? How could this be, what is happening? I'm scared John, I just want to go home now, please."

"Yes." says John. "Home … that is where you belong. Thanks for staying by my side this long doll face. There is a lot about myself that is unknown to me, I don't know why, but my past is as unclear as my future. Some of that past I was enlightened to by that fellow you clocked, thank you kindly, but what follows is now a blur. I don't know what is true and I don't know what the future brings. I know I have never in my life seen anything, anywhere that fills my heart with beauty as I look in your eyes or see you smile. It is not what I see but how I feel when I see you. Let's get you home."

Christine is listening, her head is down and John doesn't know if she hears or not, but she does. She hears the man from the airport, the man that made time stand still for a wee few hours that lasted a lifetime. Christine is done questioning herself, she doesn't need an explanation and she doesn't care why the letter bleeds or why John knows this girl. If she's nuts than she will embrace it, hell yeah … embrace it she will.

With that knowledge firmly tucked in her belt, Christine looks up at John with a smile that could fell Caesars' Army, and then she sees it. Clear as crystal she sees it.

"John," she says, "you've aged quite a bit. It is good to see you again." Christine turns to Becky to re-introduce herself. "Oh my God, John!" cries Christine as she points to where Becky was last standing.

"Becky!" yells John as he runs and kneels to her side. Becky has taken the initiative to curl up in the fetal position on the sidewalk adjacent to the Northstar Jewelry and Exchange. "Becky, are you alright?" asks John, "I mean, what's wrong Becks, are you in pain?"

"I don't feel so good." Replies Becky. "I think this girl is sick, I mean, yeah, this girl is sick. It is not good John, I'm cold and real hot all over."

"Let's get her to my place John, it is only a few miles from here, I have some stuff in my medicine cabinet, we can get her warmed up and maybe get her to a hospital or something."

"That is a start." Says John as he looks back and forth down the streets adjacent to this corner. "We need transportation."

John scoops his old hands under Becky, she is small, frail and light. John picks her up without much discomfort.

"There!" yells Christine. "A taxi … over here! Hey taxi, over here!" Christine takes a step off the curb and runs a few feet into the street with arms waving. Break lights on the taxi provides sweet relief to Christine. The taxi makes a careful u-turn and pulls up to the curb. Christine wastes no time in opening the rear door for there is no time to waste. She hops in the back to clear the way for John and the pale little girl John seems to know so well.

"412 Desert Crossing Lane." Christine says to the driver. "Do you know where that is? We are in a bit of a hurry."

"Sure do lady." Replies the driver. "I'll get you to the promised land in a jiffy."

That voice, thinks John. I know that voice. Although John is still standing on the curb, he can hear that voice all too clearly. Some things are blurry, this is not.

"Christine?" says John firmly. "Uh, could you help out and old man here? Out of the car please, just for a second so we can all get in, ok?"

"Just a second, don't go anywhere, be right back." Christine says to the driver as she confirms the length of time with her index finger while shuffling across the seat to the rear door.

"How can I help?" enquires Christine.

"Which way to your apartment?" asks John.

Christine points to the South. "Why? She asks. "We have to get going, the driver knows where we are going, he'll get us there."

"That is what I am afraid of," States John. "Thanks anyway pal. "John says to the driver of the taxi while turning to the South. "We won't be needing a ride after all, sorry for the inconvenience. Let's go Christine, I don't trust this guy." John bends both knees and makes a little jump to adjust Becky in his arms in preparation for the long haul.

John gets two steps and abruptly stops in his tracks. Christine is adjusting her purse and runs into him from behind. Up ahead, leaning against the wall of the next corner is a figure. The first thing that comes to John's mind are those black, metal ornamental figures, with one foot on the ground and the other, knee bent with the foot against an imaginary wall. You can buy these at the same place that has the chunky old lady bent over with her bloomers showing.

He would rather bloomers lady at this moment, but alas, he knows this figure, its' Max. He can smell it. John looks down at Becky in his arms. She is sick alright. He needs to get her out of this body or get her well again. If she dies here, she can't go home. The only home she has ever known. This is a strange place to her and she came to help. Thank God she is light.

"Why are we stopping?" Christine questions.

"We are not stopping." John proclaims. "We are changing direction. Trust in me Christine, we must stay North. Let's keep moving, keep your eyes open for any strange men in dark coats. Come on doll, let's go." John and Christine head North, to the

East, the sun begins to rise. To the South, the figure against the wall joins the taxi cab driver and head North as well.

John, Christine and Becky, who is being carried by John, cross the street against the blinking, do not cross sign.

"We need to get off the streets for a bit," says John. We need to get Becky some rest, it wouldn't hurt for us to get some rest too."

The city block is a mix of storefronts, restaurants and apartments. In this time of the day, the shops and eating establishments are blocked by steel gates and securely locked. The only refuge will be if an apartment door is open, surely no one will buzz them in at this time of the day.

As they walk, John sees a red and white "for rent" sign not too far ahead, just past a little bistro with wrought iron tables and chairs for customers brave enough to eat on the sidewalk. As they approach the outdoor seating area, John takes a seat in a surprisingly uncomfortable wrought iron chair, Becky sleeping on his shoulder and lap.

"Christine."

Christine crouches next to John and grasps the back of the iron chair for support. "Yeah John, how are you doing?"

"I'm fine, I need to take a break for a sec. Could you go up ahead and check some doors? Just the apartment doors, maybe one is left open of something, we need to get inside somewhere."

"No problem," replies Christine. "But I'm not going far, I am not going to leave your sight. You wait here and I will check a few of those doors down the way."

Christine walks ten feet and turns to check on John and Becky three times.

"Christine! We are fine, please," Says John as he motions down the street with his free hand.

Christine turns her palms up and shrugs, "alright," and turns to continue down the rough pavement.

John turns back to the south to see if Max is anywhere in sight, nothing, no Max, no people and no pets. No tin man, no cowardly lion and definitely no brainless straw man.

Without realizing it, in a soft lullaby John holds Becky tight and begins to sing, "You'll find he is a wiz of a wiz, if ever a wiz there was … if ever oh ever a wiz there was … the wizard of Oz is one because …"

Christine walks up the stairs to the apartment for rent, "It can't be," she says to herself. The silver lockbox hanging on the long, curved golden door handle is half open, "please be there key, please."

Christine opens the square, miniature door and removes a skeleton key from the lock box. She slowly puts the key in the lock and turns the tumblers that unlock the deadbolt. Christine opens the tall, half moon shaped entrance door and peers inside to scout their new digs, as she had hoped, the place is vacant.

"John!" she calls out, "jackpot!"

Christine stands next to John to assist him up the stairs with Becky over his now slumping right shoulder. As they enter the vacant apartment John is pleased to see the window coverings are in place and throw rugs are scattered throughout, hiding unsightly blemishes for sure. This should help them gain the needed rest as the sun begins its' assault.

John gathers three rugs, rolls them up at the end for a pillow and places them in a row, John places Becky in the middle and lies to her right, he puts one hand on her forehead, front then back as it comes to a rest on her shoulder. Christine settles herself to the opposite side of Becky, lies on her back, crosses her hands just below her chest and sleeps.

The sun moves less than a degree and this trio recedes to their dreams. The body repairs and the mind laments. John dreams he is sitting on a stool, charcoal stick in hand, sketch pad readied before him. At an angle to his left is Christine, she sits on a white rocking chair in a flowing white dress. John studies Christine then turns to the paper, eager to begin his re-creation. As his hand which holds the chalk rises to the paper, he cannot recall a single line of her face or a single flash of imagery. Almost afraid she has disappeared altogether, he quickly turns to find Christine in the exact position, sitting quietly on a white rocking chair. He studies her ever more deeply, turns to the blank white pad, raises the chalk and stops … there is nothing.

Christine finds herself lying in a comfortable bed staring at a sterile white ceiling. In slow motion, she turns down the blankets, sits up from the bed and walks out the door in a light blue speckled hospital gown. As she walks down an empty hall, Christine passes a large window that provides a crystal clear gallery view of the baby room. Perfect rows of babies snuggled quietly in old fashioned straw baskets with handles like rainbows over their inhabitants. Christine's smile fades as she looks to the back of the room, there in the back, red and white checkered nurses methodically pick up each basket by the rainbow handle and place the basket neatly inside a square box painted on the black rubber of a conveyer belt. There is no sense of danger, Christine is more intrigued than horrified. Like the stages of a car wash, Christine moves down the hall to the next window, there the conveyer deposits each basket into a yellow plastic slide that descends as it curves and winds, each basket remaining the same distance apart. At the bottom of the slide, each basket settles calmly into a river of deep green water. Christine walks slowly to the last window, presses her palms to the glass and rests her forehead in between them. It is very serene and peaceful as each basket and its' cargo float quietly into the sunset.

Becky has been dreaming for quite some time now. It's the same one, over and over. In a place where the sun is always overhead, Becky sits at the top of a grassy hill, a gazebo overlooking a crystal clear pond and playground park in front of her; train tracks bordering an endless field behind her. She sits in silence, arms crossed around her shins looking upon the park setting. There is a black paved road between her hill and the park, the signs along the road read "thanks for fishing" and "pets welcome." Becky can hear the sweet hum of a gleaming silver train approaching. The bright reflection of the train rests comfortably around Becky as it comes to a stop at the foot of the hill. Patrick, Jennifer and Mike make their way out of the train, run up the hill and join Becky's side … quietly overlooking the park.

#16 Will you take this man?

The Sun rises, the Sun sets.

Three lost souls are no quartet.

Who might the missing soul be?

Read on my friends and you will see.

As the sun settles in the center of the sky, Christine peers through the blinds to check the status of the day. The city is calm for a Saturday, slow moving vehicles pass by as if the passengers are too lazy to walk while they window shop.

John turns to Christine while he checks on Becky, "How you feelin' this morning?"

"Been better," she replies, "how's little girl doing?"

"She seems ok, but no better. We should try to get her to eat something, nothing big, maybe some bread or something."

"I agree." Christine confirms as she makes one last check through the blinds.

John supports Becky's head and picks her up to his shoulder position, which is where he is most comfortable.

Christine exits their temporary home first and waits for them at the bottom of the steps. As John closes the door behind him, he notices something peculiar. It appeared the building had been recently rehabbed, probably in preparation for renting, with a fresh coat of paint on the inside as well as the outside. The paint looks strange, from the center of the door to the left is shiny and new, to the right, it is faded and grey. As John looks at the door itself, the same phenomenon has grayed or discolored half the door.

John, Christine and Becky head North in search of bread. As they walk the occasional pedestrian gives a quick glance to the oddness of three very tired individuals from three different worlds. John realizes he has been carrying Becky for only a short time this morning but it feels like centuries. John feels as though he is walking in sand and the rising sun is growing hot.

"There." John throws his head in the direction of a church steeple he can see over the top of a building two blocks up. Let's get to that church, maybe we can get someone to check out Becks or call for medical help, something"

"Sounds good." Confirms Christine. "How are you doing, you hanging in there? We'll have to cross over, let's do it at this light."

Christine and John head towards the intersection, Christine looks both ways just as she was taught from childhood. One look to the North down the street and one look to the South down the street. In unison, John does the same. As he looks South, something strikes him as odd. The people, they all appear to be wearing the same thing, long black coats and a black hat; and another thing strikes him as odd, everyone is walking in the same direction, towards them.

John then looks North again, as if in a dream. Everyone to the North of them is just as it should be. Mom and dads, kids, some in skirts and some in shorts…it is warm he thinks. People are moving in all directions, life looks normal. Joh looks to the South, then to the North again. He notices the need to squint a little when looking

North, but not so much to the South. It just seems a bit … grayer for some reason.

This all takes but a few moments in time, a few casual glances up and down a street. "You see that?" John asks Christine. "See what?" She Replies. "The people…all the people wearing the same thing, the hats, the coats." "John, umm…I don't know what you're talking about, they all seem to be in a hurry but…that's normal, you know how it is these days, rush rush."

It doesn't take John long to determine Christine does not see the figures the way John sees the figures. That the true face of evil isn't evident on the outside and although they all appear normal, John is seeing their souls. There is danger in those souls and John knows it. John has almost forgotten the girl her cradles in his arms, Becks is motionless.

"Run!" John yells as he gathers up the energy to race across the street with Becky bouncing up and down in John's arms. "Get to the church!" he yells. "Don't wait for me, get to the church!"

"I'm staying with you and Becky!" yells Christine. "I am staying until the end!"

As if out of nowhere the group is surrounded, a circle of clones in black hats, faces in shadows angled towards the earth, hands deep in pockets. From the outside the pockets bulge and writhe as if filled with angry snakes.

John slowly and deliberately sets Becky softly to the ground. Within the circle Max stands but a few feet from John, hands outstretched as if welcoming a vampire into your home for the first time. He towers over the other Max's. Becky lies in between Max and John, Christine is tucked closely to John's left shoulder. She is frightened.

Arms still outstretched, Max snaps fingers on both hands and points to the girl. "Take the girl." He commands. Immediately, one clone from the left and one from the right ascend on Becky. As they reach down to pick her up John touches the shoulder of the clone to the right, looks into the shadowed, faceless figure. "Don't do this." John pleas. The figure pauses.

"Don't touch him!" Yells max. "Take the girl!" John recalls seeing old film, the ones where they showed newsreels of the war during feature films back in the forties. How they would flicker in black and white. This...this is exactly what is happening under the cold brim of the faceless man. A sad face is flickering in and out. John kneels beside the man, places his other hand on his shoulder and pleas once again. "Don't do this, she is an innocent little girl." The flickering intensifies, first the face, then the hat, the jacket, then the boots. Within moments, the clone is gone. In its' place is a sad, scared, middle aged man in a blue, pin striped business suit, red tie and all. This man, calmly looks and John with a boyish smile, then…once recognizing his surrounding becomes confused and scared once again…who wouldn't. The figure, now a man, runs off down the nearest alley.

There is a loud, thunderous roar from behind the circle. John and Christine turn to see what the source of this commotion is. During the confusion, Max scoops up the small shape lying before him. Unbeknownst to John and Christine as they stand in awe at what is approaching.

What appears to be riding on a bed of steam or a fog like smoke is a shiny brilliant white locomotive. This monstrous vehicle is trailed by several gleaming passenger cars, chrome accents reflect the light forcing John and Christine to shield their eyes from the reflection. Poisonous, black smoke pours out of the engine, this does not however cause one stain, not one spot of dirt or grime on the spotless finish of the locomotive.

"John! On no! Becky!" Christine points to the first passenger car, directly behind the engine. Max and several clones are boarding the train with Becky still motionless. The door closes behind them.

"Christine," John calmly addresses the woman by his side. She is disheveled, her face is dirty and her hair is wildly in all directions. She has never looked more beautiful. She looks back at John and is calm and confident as well. "If you were anybody else I would tell you to go seek refuge at that church back there. That it is too dangerous. This is my battle and I will see it to the end. But…" John pauses, looks at the ground and to the train. The poisonous smoke is intensifying. John knows there is not much time until it begins its' trek to God knows where with precious little Becks within its' wicked bowels. John looks back toward Christine. "I can't do this without you. I'm not me, I'm not strong and everything is wrong if you are not by my side. I'm sorry, I can't explain it. I just know that…together…if we go in there, we have a chance. Becky has a chance. If I go in there without you, I fear all is lost. I dunno, its' like we've been together a thousand lifetimes."

Christine does not utter a word. John doesn't need affirmation. There is no awkward silence, no longing for reassurance. There is an understanding that goes beyond typical human interaction. In this lifetime John and Christine were strangers not long ago, partners now until the end. Trust in each other that is without question, any result, including death would be shared between the two.

They turn and run toward the steam ship, whistle blowing in a ghostly cry of pain. As the train pulls away John and Christine run even faster, arms pumping and gasping for air the take an angle that should get them to the last car, a curvy twisted mangle of metal that strangely resembles a clown smile. This last car, this child nightmare incarnate has a platform completely around it, with a ladder at the rear.

Our heroes reach this back access without much trouble before the train gathers enough speed to make it impossible. John gives Christine a slight lift to the bottom rung of the iron ladder, he is able to jump and hang on to the lowest step while Christine makes her way to the top of the platform. One foot on and one off, John holds on with one hand without any real purpose and leans back to look down the street where they began pursuit. He can still see the Church they intended to take Becky, it doesn't even appear farther away, and he can see the people gathered outside. Nothing…they go about their business as if nothing is happening. Except for one man, one elderly gentleman at the top of the stairs…intently focused on the events of the day.

John makes his way to the platform where Christine awaits. "C'mon." He takes her hand and leads the way to the next car. There is but a small step between and is not difficult. It is a standard passenger car style, now it doesn't appear as sparkling and new as before. The shimmer has faded. John opens the door, still holding Christine's hand; he does not have a choice at the moment. The car is dark as they enter, well…dimly lit along the center path they move slowly into the car.

The passenger car contains no passengers, no seats or signs of life at all, just a musty smell of an ancient attic with a hint of bitterness. As they move forward a slight shimmer of light appears against the walls on both sides. Like an old black and white movie shown on reel to reel, it flickers and is dull. Images begin to appear, not quite sure of their content, they are an angry image, which is quite clear.

As John and Christine continue forward the images clarify, men fighting, ancient beasts of unknown origin, gnashing teeth, horns and twisting motions. There are no sounds, thankfully, for John fears if sounds accompanied these images he would surely go mad.

Christine stays close to John, her left shoulder firmly pressed to John's right shoulder blade, hands clenched, she fears not. "Resolute of the intrepid!" These words ring within Christine's ears. Her grandfather used to spew these words at every triumphant moment. He would raise his fist in the air and loudly proclaim, "Resolute of the intrepid!" Long ago summer days in granddads back yard, watching her young cousins learn to play wiffle ball, granddad underhand slow pitching to two young lads. Each swing of the bat, each unforgettable "whap" of the wiffle ball, "Resolute of the intrepid!" It was gibberish to us, it was the meaningless craw of an old timer. It still doesn't make much sense but wherever it originated, it had real meaning. Christine, after her grandfather's death looked up the words to make meaning of the phrase. She was twelve years old at the time. She remembers wishing she had asked granddad why those words had such meaning to him.

John is undeterred, they continue forward. With each step Christine goes back, she is twelve again. She is alone under the stairs at her school. It is lunchtime. She has no food for lunch or money to buy it and is embarrassed. From under the stairs windows floor to ceiling allow Christine to look out to the busy street just beyond the green manicured perfection of academia.

Anybody…Christine remembers with a heavy heart…anybody at all. Anybody but herself, she was jealous of the lives of every passerby, regardless of the pain and suffering that may exist. Those were hard times, they didn't last forever and Christine has grown over the years. She doesn't realize it but she has become a healer in all definitions of the word… her true calling.

The shell of the train is seemingly becoming transparent. The mist gives way to a visual of the outside. They speed along at what seems an impossible rate to maintain. Continuing to walk both John and Christine can't help but remain transfixed on their surroundings. It's as if they gone back in time as they relentlessly go into their future.

The images are clearer, the unrecognizable beasts have become men, teeth still gnashing and screams as fierce as before, they are men nonetheless. These men wear armor, battling each other in the name of God.

John never loses site of their destination, Becky is up there, somewhere and she needs a savior. They come to the door at the front of this unlikely and most heinous time machine, John pulls it aside to reveal a platform between the two cars. Before stepping out they look down onto a pitted and rusty chrome platform...to their amazement they realized the locomotive is not moving. They slowly step out and look back toward where they once stood as Max and his doubles surrounded them. John can still see the Church, the crowd of people and the lone elder man staring back at them. They haven't moved an inch.

"What the?" mutters Christine. John puts his index and middle finger to Christine's lips cutting her off. "Yeah" he says, "Did you pull the emergency breaks when I wasn't lookin?" Christine smiles a sweet crooked smile and put her left hand to John's cheek. "You're a funny, freaky old man, but I like you anyway." "Thanks doll." John softly says. "You ready for door number two?"

Johns pulls this door aside and begins to enter. As he does he glimpses back to the church, somehow he knew he was still being watched and he wasn't wrong. As they enter, they enter a still speeding locomotive, bent on hurling itself through the bowels of time. No mist this time, clear images speeding through time with a sense of unjust righteousness. People he recognized from the history books, doing unspeakable things, people he did not recognize from the history books doing unspeakable things under the mask of morality.

All of them, they all had a chance, he can see this somehow. They had a chance to do the right thing, they had a chance to be healers, every one of them. Some blamed others, some blamed themselves and the weaknesses within, others sought to shelter their decisions under the cover of human emotions. They all had a chance.

John and Christine moved through this car with a heightened speed and awareness, coming upon the next door just short of abruptly. In a single action John pulls this door aside and does not bother checking the step or looking to see if his watcher remains. If he did so he would see this platform has decayed to black rotted steel. The door is also black and rotted, this once shiny train has become a festering dungeon on wheels.

John keeps Christine close as they enter the darkness of the third car.

#17 Yes, I see can the clarity in your fog

Darkness, of course, why should this be any different? What was he expecting, a brass band, a big top with a bunch of elephants and a bear on a bicycle? Seriously, John thinks to himself. Seriously? Just then the train lurches, as if someone pulled the emergency cord for a second then let it go with an "oops!" This sends John and Christine suddenly forward and instantly back.

John grabs Christine as they tumble back and pulls her on top of him to ease her impact. The two crash to the floor just in front of the rear door. The way down is not without interruption as John's head hits a brass kick stop sticking out of that very exit. There is no light to fade, darkness gives way to darkness as John fades. He can hear Christine's voice like she is falling down a bottomless canyon. "John!" she screams, "John…."

A firm, commanding, in control voice replaces Christine. "John..wake up my boy." John slowly opens his sleep encrusted eyes. Instinctively uses both index fingers to grind the sleep bunnies away. You can't wake up till they're gone right? "Hey dad." He responds with a deep sigh, the somber, deep sigh of comfort and safety, followed by a moan of contentment. "How's my boy? You sleep well?" "Yeah dad, what's up?" "I gotta go outta town bud, just be a day, k? wanted to say goodbye, tell you I love you." "That's cool," says John with a stretch, "Tomorrow right?" His dad replies, "Yes, bud, tomorrow," "Hey, real quick. I was thinkin." John's dad gives his typical grin, he knows what's coming and John grins back because he knows very well too. "So I was thinkin, if God exists…why…? Why do I hurt sometimes, why do good people suffer? I don't understand, it doesn't make any sense. And what was here before? Who created God, How could he have always been here? Dad…I just don't get it.

If one never questions faith, the truly devout, it's quite rare. Most that don't question do so not on devotion but on guilt or fear, don't see the true depth of faith. If you are too afraid to doubt, then you are too afraid to really believe. Grow…learn, love. How does this happen if you have never questioned. There is no teacher so knowledgeable that can preach to a student all-encompassing truth, we are not capable of that and those so bold to proclaim such should be dismissed for the act of proclamation. There is no student that can learn from the most talented teacher than will never query. Query on, never stop questioning, believe in what is true and just in the depth of your soul and never be afraid. That is where the truth lies.

John's father loves to tell stories. It frustrates some but John loves his dads' stories. What is frustrating is they don't always make sense. They seem to make sense to him, but…not always the balance of the room. John doesn't care, he just likes to hear him talk, the passion in his voice, the faith his dad believes in the words he speaks. "Well me boy," he begins, "A man I have known, World War 1 veteran, a surgeon. An old man, quite old enough to be considered an infant of mortality came to me one day. He sat, like this." His father raises his right hand, thumb to forefinger and middle finger join as they have for generations, raises his hand in the air as the old Italians always do in question. "This old man waves his hand to me in a gesture I hope lives on in eternity my boy, then poses the eternal question. He says, "Last night, I was watchin a show, brilliant tv show, just wonderful. The big bang theory. Very interesting. Why?" He says. "Why did it take God so long to make us? Billions of years since the Universe was created. What was he doing? Where was he?"

John's dad pauses. "Now you have to understand, this man served in World War II, a religious old Italian Catholic. He was 92 years old when he asked me this. These are questions from a man of great knowledge in the possible waning days of his life. I have to think God respects and appreciates this type of faith. Not being afraid to ask without ever abandoning your beliefs. Why my boy? I can't answer that for you. I am glad you asked though."

The darkness is replaced by darkness. "John? John, wake up, please…Are you ok?" Tenderness and love are replaced by tenderness and love. The warmth of Johns' bed is replaced by the stench of death and disease. "Yes, I'm ok. How long have I been out?" "Just a minute or so, John, you scared me, I'm scared." Panic is in her voice. "I don't know what to do? What are we gonna do, Becky…this train…or whatever we are in…John…"

John sits up, elbows on knees and fingers entwined.

"Well…looks like we have to find Becks doll, fuck this train."

Our old friends, it seems so long. Patrick, Jen and Mike have hunkered down in John's office frantically trying to figure out what is playing out before them. Patrick has pushed John's chair back and to the side to rest on his palms on the dark wooden desk. Jen has taken residence in the chair and Mike stands facing Patrick, the computer screen a rectangular metallic lifeline is between the two.

'Well? Patrick? What's goin on?" Mike asks. "Dude, nothing since they went into that old abandoned railcar. No matter what I do I can't see in it, no movement, nothing. They have been in there a long time, too long if you ask me."

Jen's fidgeting in John's chair, her fingers tapping feverishly on both her knees. The swivel is getting the workout of a lifetime. "We have to do something.' Jen adds. "I can't just sit here. Becky, John…they need us. Michael looks at Jen like he just ate a crate of lemons. "You're not serious, what are you crazy? You saw…you see what's going on down there, with Becks, with John, seriously? You have no idea who or what you're gonna be when you get there. Let alone what you are gonna do, let's just…keep an eye on things, see if we can help from here."

19 There is an island of darkness in all of us

John grabs hold of Christine's hand, "This way doll," as if there was any other way but toward the darkness. The screeching and rumbling of the train is at a feverish and chaotic precipice, the noise combined with the turbulence and swaying have become a white noise that would drive any other traveler that punched a ticket on this locomotive beyond mad.

John leads the way, Christine in tow. A dark cloud looms in this car, they both see it. The screeching and rumbling continues…increases. John enters the cloud, Christine does not. They are still holding hands as John becomes fully engulfed, he pauses…he turns to Christine, they both know she cannot enter. John begins to weep, he doesn't know why. He just knows he is alone in the world at this moment; the feeling is catastrophic and welcoming at the same time. They slowly release the grip that has tied them together this entire time, faith ties their bond but uncertainty chews at the stitches.

The palms relax, the fingers slowly glide along true loves outstretches hands. Fingertips take one last fatal gasp. Then…John's arms settle at his side. He is looking neither forward nor back. He doubts everything. The sounds of the train are gone. Christine is in the past, as all things are. The future doesn't exist, the present is but for a moment and our entire lives are made up of the past.

As John remains in the darkness the doubt continues to overtake him. The loneliness begins to possess him. The loneliness turns to anger, Johns screams out, "Why!" He throws a fist in the air and screams again, "Why, dammit!" and falls to his knees. The anger and loneliness becomes anguish and an odd love for the pain in his soul. There is a comfort in the pain; John's soul is on fire with regret, loss, hate, suffrage and an unyielding love.

John remains on his knees, chin to chest with arms by his side. He hears Christine's voice, "John! Please John, let me in!" He shakes his head slowly, "Can't love," John mutters, "Can't."

John takes a deep breath, another…distinctive voice resonates from the bowels of the darkness. "Alone you shall sit, alone you shall be, until you brace me John, if you think they know you, all you've dreamed and all you've desired…you are fooling yourself!" The sound of poisoned laughter accompanies Max's words, "They don't know you John, nor do they care! Seriously, look at yourself, where are they now! Here you are, on your knees…pathetic…you're nobody…join me John. Be somebody, Be a man, not some pathetic boy in a man's body.'

A distant voice rings in John's ears, faint, fleeting. Softly in the distance…"John…can you hear me, its' Christine, please John…please let me in…"

Still on his knees, hands now folded in front of him, in the now present deafening silence, a familiar, soft voice kindly speaks. John looks up and sees Jen, sweet little Jen. "I miss my Dad. I watched him cry alone in his truck every morning for a month after my…after I was gone. He laid his head on the steering wheel and cried till the tears could no longer come. He would drive to work and not remember a moment of it as he was lost in his sorrow. I was his little girl.

"One day he pulled his truck to the side of the road, it was a windy street he travelled every day for years. Nothing special, corn fields on both sides with a huge billboard that could be seen for miles touting "R Place Truck Stop! Cleanest Restrooms this side of the Mississippi!" He pulled over, got out of his truck and wandered into the field. It was Fall and the corn had been harvested, short shards of stalks jetted out and my dad was kinda stumbling around, through the short stalks. He stopped…just like you right now John…he fell to his knees. He wasn't crying anymore. He looked to the sky…he looked right at me. He said…"I love you my baby…I miss you, I live for you. I will always…live for you." He blew me a kiss stood up and walked back to his truck the man I always knew and loved. My dad…"

Jen knelt down before John and placed her palm on his forehead. John reached up and placed his palm on the back of her hand and pressed down. Still on his knees, He squeezes her hand and pulls it to his lips and gently kisses the back of her hand, "Thanks Jen, you have saved us both…me…and your loving father."

"Let's go." John gently tugs Jen's hand as he leads her deeper into the darkness of the cloud, which now swirls like an angry tornado, clouds of teeth gnashing at the pair as they descend. Descend they do, darkness has evolved to eternal blackness, the rumble and the rage of the locomotive has long since been drowned out by the tormented screams of the black.

John leads and Jen follows, as if a roadmap in his mind leads the way. John feels comfortable about this and a faint grin emerges from the expression of determination. Images of a child, waking in the dark of his home, making his way in the middle of the night to use the bathroom. Mom hadn't rearranged the furniture in a decade, John could easily navigate his way without a morsel of light.

John stops, Jen in pace, John slowly extends his hand and feels the bitter cold of an ancient, steel door handle. Without hesitation Johns turns the handle to disengage the latch that stands between the two and what lies on the otherworldly side of this nightmare. Neither John nor Jen any longer hear the howls and the gnashing that continues to feed upon them. As John crack open the door, the howling is replaced by a tremendous sucking sounds that devours the darkness, in an instant. The door is cracked maybe an inch, John and Jen stand silent in an equally silent but dismal railroad car.

#20 Truth is in the eye of the be-deviler

John looks bashfully to Jen, shrugs…"didn't see that coming…you?" "Nope," and shrugs back. John puts a finger in his ear and twists it around as if cleaning the last of the decrepit sounds from his ears. "Well, shall we?"…Jen replies, "We shall."

John takes Jen by the hand, squeezes tightly, Jen is comforted. She doesn't know what lies ahead. A gentle squeeze of the hand has no answers, predicts no futures. She is not alone, that is all that matters.

There is a sense of closeness, finality. John can feel it, a tingling, a spidey sense…the roar of the train…the images and craziness has been replaced by normality. John and Jen face what John feels is curtain number 3. "Price is right Max. Let's see whatya got."

The handle is not a handle, the door knob is not a door knob. The pair looks down on this lever to a gateway that in their hearts is sure to lead them to a place that ends this nightmare. For good or bad, the end. Little do they know the end is closer than they know. Not an end they envision, but an end to all humanity.

The door is round, wood with raised spirals, large on the outside and continue in a circle until disappearing in the center of the door. Rusty barbed wire shadows the raised spirals like a flesh eating, bloody fence around a simple child's maze. In this center is the handle like creature, John and Jen stare in amazement. It is definitely a knob, it will without a doubt open this door. Maintaining the shape of a large door knob, twisting and writhing, black snakes with pitchfork tongues hissing and calling his name. Between them, razor sharp spikes jet out, on the ends of the spikes are three blades, in the shape of a cross.

"This is it Jen," John calmly looks to Jen. "You good?" Without hesitation Jen looks to the center of the door, then back to John, "All in." With a quick but reassuring nod, John places his hand on the knob, the snakes turn to stone, the crosses of blades to not cut…as John turns the door knob, the door does not open but simply turns to dust.

#21 There is a man on the corner of Broadway and 5<u>th</u>. He has a

sign draped over his shoulders that says "The end is Near" He is

correct.

Patrick and Mike have not moved, they have not breathed, they have not uttered a word. The images on the screen are incomprehensible. They have seen so much, so much over the afterlifetime…What they see now, they cannot comprehend. The train, racing on the tracks, their loved compatriots fighting for their lives. Against who, what…and why. It's craziness.

The locomotive that contained so many twisted and ugly railcars is now down to two. The speed has reached ridiculous levels. A black locomotive surrounded by a sea of grey, seeming to suck all life around it like a black hole. All that once made sense…streets, buildings, infinite rows of corn on a midwest plain. A beautiful crop of wine grapes on a Napa Valley Hillside…gone. Now, Patrick and Mike view a locomotive missile, heading through those streets that they know so well, but beyond those streets…what always seemed like never-ending tracks…nothing.

The screen shows only static. If the train reaches the end of the track. It enters oblivion…and with it…so do we.

#22 Outta my way Bro:

Brothers in arms, Brothers can say, trust me Brother, for there is no other way.

The boys' race…as boys do. They race, they wrestle. Boys dance a silly dance when victory is achieved. Fingers point to the sky, muscles twitch and noses flair. Boys fight, boys become men. These boys never became men, not in an earthly way. Right now…they run. They run to the door that leads them to a fight…to a cause that has led many boys…and men…to the darkness. Leaving behind everything and not accounting for the consequence, for it has neither judge nor jury here, for the love and the truth of the destination.

They run. As diligent is the train speeding to oblivion…industrious is our boys. They run in unison, they run to the door. The door in the past was an obstacle, an aversion. The door was something to be afraid of. Something to avoid…to fear.

Now, the door is an object to be conquered, no army shall stand in the way. Mike and Patrick plunge through the door and into total darkness.

Within the same slow sweet exhale, John and Jen open the door and willingly enter into the black. "Mike, are you here?" "Yeah," Patrick replies, "Wherever here is." "Jen, hold my hand. I can't see anything." Without a word Jen, already clutching John's hand squeezes ever so tightly. Soft sweet words follow in the next soft sweet exhale, Jen…under her breathe whispers, "God..let there be light."

Light by definition is not always physically luminous. When one enters a room, flicks a switch and, presto! Light. Opening those room darkening curtains…bam! Blinding light. Staring at that ridiculous word problem in math…what the? Then suddenly…there it is, "oh yeah, I get it."

Well, this is all of them combined and wrapped up in a tidy atomic bomb. The four of them stand in the railcar. Mike, Patrick, Jen and John. They can't see each other but they know they are there. It is still utter darkness. They also know they are not alone, that Becky and Christine are there as well. Two other unwelcome and lowly guests have made themselves at home. But then again, they are not the guests, they are home. Max…and his side kick. The end of time.

"Max!" John shouts. "Maaax!" even louder. Slowly…physical illumination fills the room. This is the end of the road, so to speak, the last railcar, the engine. It's large, two stories large, Mike and Patrick are crouched in the middle of the room, and they turn to look at John and Jen. John is in front of Jen, shielding her, at the opposite end of the freight car. Max is at the helm, on the upper level overlooking the tracks as the train speeds toward oblivion. The tracks are now made of bones but John can clearly see through the single front window that the city they are terrorizing is still that of the town Christine used to reside in.

At the helm with Max is Becky, she lies lifeless, knees tucked to her chest on a bale of hay at Max's side. Directly below is Christine, sitting on the bottom rung of a spiral staircase that leads up to the helm, wearing a white dress, elbows on knees and face in her hands. She has no idea what's going on. She is lost.

John calls out to her. Christine slowly turns to look, sees John at the other end of the car and runs to him. Mike and Patrick step back as Christine runs directly between them as if they didn't exist and jumps into Johns arms. They join her, not in John's arms but at his side. This is the first time they are all together, but missing one thing, Becks.

Mike looks at John with desperation, "John…this train." "I know." Says John. Remember that illumination thing? They don't know why, but they know. They all know what this train is heading toward. That they have to get off of it, that they need to get off as a group, with Becky or into the abyss together.

Together, as with the word light has so many meanings. We plow through life, together, because we all do. Whether we want to or not, no matter how alone you feel at any time, you can't abandoned the world which we live. We are all together in this thing. On an elevator, strangers group together, at work or school, together, with a common purpose and an individual agenda, all at the same time.

Blood binds, our brothers and sisters, our mothers and fathers…our children. Many of us would die to protect the blood of our own. For far too many it ends there. There are heroes yes, countless heroes in this world, but the gap, the divide is tremendous. The blood of our heroes courses through their veins as the blood of the whole. That blood has not forgotten we have all come from one father. Heroes die for strangers, because in that blood we are all brothers, sisters, mothers fathers and most of all…children.

Together they stand, our heroes, bound by faith and all that is true. Their blood parted ways thousands of years ago, but remains strong for it was built on an unbreakable foundation, to be brought down only by those that built it.

#23 She was the light, the way…the one…someday…for us all you live, for us all you die

Harmony, sweet harmony

Your song shall never end

I hear your melody in every breathe I take

In sleep, in death…my friend

This trip has lasted way to long. Nobody punched a ticket, nobody checked any bags. Who is running this show anyway? The time is now, its' not high noon but John knows the showdown must commence. The locomotive screams passed newly built, brightly painted row house type buildings that turn grey in our wake. John can faintly make out an old church at the end of the road, with a back scape filled with blackness. That's the end of the road, literally.

Max knows it too, he needs to take this team with him into the black, there he finds victory…there…he can bind their souls in the darkness for eternity, taking this world with it. The platform slowly lowers, a shallow whining of gears fills the silent room. Max's stare never leaves Johns' face, for he has one goal. Max has not been this close for over 2,000 years.

With poor Becks lying in stillness at the feet of this monster, she seems at peace. Either knowing her savior is upon her or it will be in the afterlife regardless of the outcome. Max reaches down and picks her up, effortlessly with one arm he cradles her at his side.

John takes a step forward and is quickly blocked by Christine. Christine takes a half a step and puts her arm in front of John. "No." she says as she gazes up to meet Johns' eyes. An army of raging bulls could not have stopped John from confronting Max for the sake of sweet, defenseless Becky. One small hand and wide eyes of Christine cement Johns' feet to the floor.

Christine slowly shakes her head, "No." She whispers. Christine gently raises her right hand to touch Johns' cheek, caresses it softly. "We will have our time John. Trust in me…trust in you. If you do that for me, forever is only but a moment away."

The train continues to race, toward complete insanity, chaos, blackness and what is now the faint chorus of twisting and screaming souls. The rail which this train rides is now bones that twist and writhe like a blender, devouring all that lay upon it. Max watches intensely, ready to take on John for that has been his sole purpose. To use Becky as a pawn in his game, he just needs to buy a little more time, to distract John until it is too late.

Christine can see it…it is but a moment. A moment is all that's needed. The eyes are a truly a window to the soul. John trusts her, with everything. He does not know why but he does. In this moment, like standing in the middle of a tornado surrounded by a hurricane during a snowstorm, John is warm.

Christine turns from John…but also for John and everything he stands for. Max, with a startled and bemused look sees Christine turn and run directly towards him and Becky. In an instant he knows he underestimated this. That he focused on John too much, that he underestimated humanity in a white dress.

Max raises Becky above his head, in an effort to launch her at his invader. Christine is now only a few feet away. Christine runs, with her greatest effort throws herself into Max's midsection. Max loses his grip on Becky as she falls to the ground in a soft bundle of flesh, almost how she came into this world. John Screams and reaches out, as if to grip someone going over a ledge from 40 feet away. Knowing its' impossible but reaching out nonetheless.

Christine propels Max backward, crashing through the glass on the front of the train. Max and Christine disappear into the rails that are a grinder of bones. John, Jen, Mike and Patrick race to the front of the car. The boys tend to Becky as John runs to the shattered remains of the railcars' front window. Hope, desperation? Until the end…but she is gone. John puts both hands on the metal base where the glass was bonded to the train and looks over the edge with a heavy heart. Nothing, the train has stopped and the rails are steel again.

John looks up from the tracks, a short distance ahead is the church he saw from a distance, behind him Patrick has picked up a lifeless Becky and Mike looks to John for what is next.

"Let's go." Commands John. "Off this train, we need to save Becks. You got her?"

"Yeah, I'm good." Patrick replies. They follow John to the side of the train where the exit and a short metal staircase leads them to into a muggy summer day.

There is no need to look back, there are no faces to look back to. Up ahead, John can see the steps to the church. There are many and he can't see them all, only the top steps. The lower steps are full, a crowd of some sort milling around outside the steps. As they get closer, through the sweat, John can see the crowd is well dressed. Very well dressed, tuxes and flowing dresses fill the landscape. People are talking and laughing in a general festive atmosphere.

John realizes a wedding is soon to commence. Good for them, what a happy day. John, Jen and the boys stop running as they reach the curb on the corner of the church, John can see the name written in a large stone plaque on the corner, St Mary's Catholic Church.

Several tuxedoed gentlemen are standing in a group and can't help but notice the arrival of these uninvited guests.

The eldest of the group approaches John and his cargo. "Hey, is your little girl ok? She doesn't look well, let's get her inside, out of this oppressive heat."

Before the elder can finish his statement they carry Becky begin to be ushered up the steps to the church by well-dressed female wedding attendees. The large double doors are opened as an invitation to all. All that wish to enter … all that choose to enter. That is a critical decision, for wishing to enter will not get you across the threshold.

The church is full, all pews are locked and loaded in anticipation of today's events. The polite chatter has grown silent as all eyes turn to them.

"We need some place to lay her down." Patrick says to John.

"Up there, keep walking." replies John. "The steps to the alter are carpeted, we can put her down there."

As John and the crew progress down the aisle, the wedding guests rise for a better look. This is not what they expected, but this is a wedding, anything can happen on this day. When John is halfway down the aisle the men on the stairs fill the back of the church.

They reach the altar and slowly place Becky on the soft carpet. Jen now crying … Becky is lifeless.

John, on his knees looks up to the congregation, spreads open his arms and pleads, "Can no one help us? We need to save this girl!"

Patrick and Mike look up at John as he makes this plea for salvation, from the lowest step, Jen on her knees just in front of the boys, Becky in the middle and John at the foot of the altar with a large crucifix hanging in front of leaded glass just behind him.

Jen, gasping for air, is crying for a different reason now. She cannot speak but can see the eyes … His eyes. The eyes of the man that gave his life on the cross and the eyes of the man at the foot of the altar, they are the same. The face, older yes, but the face is undeniable. Somewhere far, far away, Christine and all in her world bow down.

No one speaks, the church remains silent. John looks around, and then looks to the sky. "God." He says softly. "Don't leave Becky here. Just this one time, make an exception, take her home. Please, God, please father. Take her home."

In the silence, footsteps down the center aisle emerge. The elder in the tuxedo approaches. The footsteps are deafening and end at the base of the steps to the altar. "I have missed you, my boy." The elder crouches next to Becky and lays a lone, soft hand to her forehead. A white, burning light slowly outlines Becks' body and becomes increasingly bright until her image fades with the light itself.

"Go home my love." Says the elder.

John looks on with a boyish fascination and reverence for this man, for his father … his dad.

"It is time, my son, time for you to become the man I know you are. This world needs you, my time has moved on."

"But dad, I don't want you to go, please stay." John begins to cry. Jen can see the boy in a grown man's face. "We haven't had any time, what am I supposed to do?"

The Father goes to his son, hugs him softly as only a father can and gently strokes his son's head with his right hand. The father whispers softly in his son's ear. "Do what is right, I love you very much, it is time you show this love to the rest of our children."

John takes a small step back to look at his father for the first time in so many years. "You're saying it is time for you to go … and my time to rule?" asks John, putting his hand to his chest, looking out over the church where every man, women and child has remained silent and remained on their knees.

"No, my boy, not to rule." Says the Father.

"To lead."

www.ingramcontent.com/pod-product-compliance
Lightning Source LLC
Chambersburg PA
CBHW070921130626
46555CB00001B/233